HOLD ME

(A Katie Winter FBI Suspense Thriller—Book 7)

Molly Black

Molly Black

Bestselling author Molly Black is author of the MAYA GRAY FBI suspense thriller series, comprising nine books (and counting); of the RYLIE WOLF FBI suspense thriller series, comprising six books (and counting); of the TAYLOR SAGE FBI suspense thriller series, comprising six books (and counting); and of the KATIE WINTER FBI suspense thriller series, comprising nine books (and counting).

An avid reader and lifelong fan of the mystery and thriller genres, Molly loves to hear from you, so please feel free to visit www.mollyblackauthor.com to learn more and stay in touch.

BOOKS BY MOLLY BLACK

MAYA GRAY MYSTERY SERIES
GIRL ONE: MURDER (Book #1)
GIRL TWO: TAKEN (Book #2)
GIRL THREE: TRAPPED (Book #3)
GIRL FOUR: LURED (Book #4)
GIRL FIVE: BOUND (Book #5)
GIRL SIX: FORSAKEN (Book #6)
GIRL SEVEN: CRAVED (Book #7)
GIRL EIGHT: HUNTED (Book #8)
GIRL NINE: GONE (Book #9)

RYLIE WOLF FBI SUSPENSE THRILLER
FOUND YOU (Book #1)
CAUGHT YOU (Book #2)
SEE YOU (Book #3)
WANT YOU (Book #4)
TAKE YOU (Book #5)
DARE YOU (Book #6)

TAYLOR SAGE FBI SUSPENSE THRILLER
DON'T LOOK (Book #1)
DON'T BREATHE (Book #2)
DON'T RUN (Book #3)
DON'T FLINCH (Book #4)
DON'T REMEMBER (Book #5)
DON'T TELL (Book #6)

KATIE WINTER FBI SUSPENSE THRILLER
SAVE ME (Book #1)
REACH ME (Book #2)
HIDE ME (Book #3)
BELIEVE ME (Book #4)
HELP ME (Book #5)
FORGET ME (Book #6)
HOLD ME (Book #7)
PROTECT ME (Book #8)
REMEMBER ME (Book #9)

PROLOGUE

Sherrie Blair was panting for breath. She ran, terrified, taking a headlong route into the darkness. Bruised from the fall, her knees skinned, her hands bleeding from the struggle to escape, she couldn't believe she'd gotten away.

He had held her prisoner. For a long time. Many hours.

"I'm going to kill you," he'd promised her when she'd screamed to be let out. "Just like all the others. I'm sorry. You're not working out. You have to die."

She remembered how strange, how implacable his voice had sounded, and reliving those creepy words now gave her the strength to start running even faster.

She had no idea where she was. It was in the middle of nowhere and it was an utterly dark night. She was forging her way through deep, uneven snow. Pine trees towered above her and the air felt fresh and icy cold.

Stars blanketed the night sky, frigid pinpricks in the blackness.

Wind blew around her, cold as steel.

She knew she had escaped into an icy world of nothing where danger lurked. It could be deadly, but anything - anything - was better than being locked in that cage to wait until he made good on his threats.

The problem was that she was now entirely lost. And it was freezing.

Sherrie whimpered. She was so cold. Achingly cold. She'd had only a light jacket on when he'd taken her. She hadn't expected to be out in these frigid temperatures.

She stumbled and fell, twisting her ankle, then got up and kept on at a limping run, slipping on the snow, falling, getting up to run again. She wove through the trees, but now she was realizing that hiding was pointless. She couldn't hear anyone behind her and didn't think he was chasing after her.

But there was nothing around except darkness.

Trees surrounded her, their trucks cold, their branches festooned with snow. Ice crunched under her feet.

She was shuddering with cold.

"You have to find a road," she told herself. "Or a house. You have to find shelter."

She listened, but could hear nothing. The utter silence was broken only by the whisper of the wind in the branches.

As she stumbled along, trying her best to work out where she'd come from and where she should go, Sherrie realized she was utterly disoriented.

She'd escaped him, she'd gotten away from her captor. But now, another enemy surrounded her, its icy fingers clutching at her, sapping her strength and burning her skin.

The cold.

The cold would kill her and he'd known that. Perhaps it was why he hadn't chased after her for as long as she'd feared. She had to get help. But it was hard to move.

Sherrie stumbled forward, quaking with the chill, unable to feel her hands and feet as she wove her way through the icy trees.

"Let me find a road," she told herself. "Let me find a house."

But there was only the dark forest, swallowing her up.

With her limbs quaking, the ice invading the core of her body, Sherrie feared that soon, her hiding place would become her tomb.

CHAPTER ONE

Katie Winter knocked on the front door of her old family home. Emotions stormed inside her as she waited. At least, this time she knew the door would be opened. Her parents would not ignore her, refusing to acknowledge her presence outside.

Her parents were expecting her to visit, but after an estrangement of more than fifteen years, she knew it would not be a calm or easy meeting. Also, she was keeping secrets - from both of them. She pushed her brown hair back from her face, narrowing her green eyes, thinking uneasily of what could not be said.

"Good morning, Katie."

With a smile that was at least partly warm, her father came to the door to greet her. Once tall and strong, he now looked haggard, older than his years. His eyes were still piercing and bright, but his hair was gray and his shoulders were stooped.

As Katie followed him into the small home, set near the shores of Lake Ontario, she reminded herself that her father didn't know that she was looking once more into the catastrophe that had defined her life - the disappearance of her twin sister Josie.

She'd reopened the case, this time looking at it from her capacity as a seasoned FBI agent. And after interviewing her sister's suspected killer in prison, she'd come up with an unexpected lead from him. She wanted to explore it while she was back home. But she couldn't tell her parents about it. This was something she had to keep from them. For now and perhaps forever.

Katie walked into the lounge and sat down with her dad.

She didn't look at the chair Josie had always used, standing empty near the fireplace. And she knew she couldn't mention Josie. Her father would shut down. The topic was still a point of pain for him and he refused to discuss it.

"Hi, Dad," she said. "It's good to see you."

"Good to see you, too, sweetheart."

"How are you?"

"I'm fine."

"You look tired."

He shrugged. "I don't sleep well these days."

"Do you want to talk about it?" Katie asked, feeling worried, but her father shook his head.

"It's a family trait. What are you now, thirty-two? When you get to sixty, you'll likely have the same difficulty."

Finally, he gave her a resigned smile.

Katie didn't think that was the real reason, but she didn't get a chance to ask about it, because at that moment, her mother walked in, carrying a tray of coffee.

"Katie!" Her mother's face warmed, which sent a flash of emotion through her. It was weird but wonderful to have her mother happy to see her, even though in many ways, she still felt like a stranger to Katie.

Her mother knew that Katie was trying to find out more about Josie. She was desperate to be kept in the loop about what Katie discovered, and wanted to know what had happened to her daughter.

But although her mother knew she was re-looking into Josie's disappearance, she couldn't tell her everything. She didn't want to share facts that were not fully confirmed, or leads that might go nowhere. She'd rather wait, and give information that she knew was accurate.

As they stirred their coffee, the aroma filling the small lounge, Katie thought about how complex families were.

Katie glanced at her father - and she saw the loss in his eyes. He'd lost his daughter and he'd never recovered from it. Katie couldn't bear that she'd caused that loss. The guilt would haunt her forever.

Years of grief had taken their toll, and now her parents were frail; she could see that. The past was lurking in this house, a dark and ominous presence that had shaped all their lives.

Katie felt it. Her father felt it. Her mother certainly felt it.

"This is delicious," she said to her mother, trying to warm the chill that had suddenly blown in.

She knew she had to keep things light. Katie couldn't tell them what she really wanted to talk about. They were fragile; they were vulnerable. And they had their own secrets too.

In her mind, she'd rehearsed this meeting many times. She'd figured out what she could say, what she couldn't say.

"I'm glad you came," her mother said. "I've missed you."

"It's good to see you both," Katie said, and meant it.

"You're looking well. Happier," her mother said hesitantly.

"I am happy. I'm loving my job. Working with the cross-border task force is fascinating."

Katie hoped this wasn't treading too close to dangerous ground. Perhaps it wouldn't be, if she didn't discuss any actual cases.

"You were going to show me the photos of your apartment," her mother reminded her.

Katie took out her phone and scrolled through, showing her parents a few shots of the small, serene rental in Sault Ste Marie, overlooking the St. Mary's River, on the U.S. side, with a view of the Canadian side of the town.

"Isn't it lovely? Look at that view."

Her father nodded. "It's quite something. I'm sure you're too busy to enjoy it to the full, though. Knowing you."

The words were said with affection.

"Well, I hope you're not letting work get in the way of a social life." Her mother said that with a smile.

"Mom, I've never been one for socializing," Katie pointed out. And it was true. She'd always been a loner, and the trauma that had played out when she was sixteen had guided her even more strongly in that direction.

Even now, sitting with her parents, the conversation felt like hard work. There was so much hurt to be overcome. So much that couldn't be said.

"You're not still a workaholic, are you?" her mother asked.

"I'm not a workaholic. I'm dedicated to my job. That's very different."

"And have you met anyone?"

Katie smiled. "No. No, I'm not looking to get romantically involved when work's so busy."

But her thoughts went briefly to her investigation partner, Leblanc. She saw his lean, handsome, olive-skinned face in her mind. His crisp, dark hair. The air of confidence. The warmth in his eyes.

But she wasn't going to tell her parents that her feelings for him were deepening. Katie wasn't even ready to admit that to herself.

"Things like that happen when you're not looking for them," her father said sagely.

Katie smiled at him. She wished that were true. Instead, she felt like there was a whole part of her life that was outside of her control.

She didn't want to think about it. She didn't want to think about what the future might hold with Leblanc. Katie wasn't afraid of much, but the thought of an emotional commitment was a terrifying leap of faith to her.

"How's business going?" she asked. Her parents ran a boat hire company, and although Katie saw they'd scaled down some in the past few years, they were still keeping on with it.

"We still get by," her father said. "We don't work as hard as we used to. But we're not ready to give it up."

"It's starting to get busier now, as the weather warms. But spring is late this year," her mother said.

Katie was used to the bitter winds that froze the area in winter. She'd grown up with them and she'd thought nothing of them, but she could understand how the freezing temperatures could be difficult for tourists.

"True, we haven't seen much sun recently," Katie agreed.

She glanced outside. The sky was gray, the lake choppy.

Katie felt suddenly restless. And she sensed that her parents had spent enough time with her. There was only so much time that could be spent before the unspoken issues began looming.

"I'm going to take a walk into town," she said. "Can I get you anything?"

"No, we're fine," her mother said, and she noticed the glance that passed between her parents. They suspected she wasn't going into town just for the walk. Katie felt sure of it.

But nobody was saying anything. Just thinking it.

"Thanks for the coffee," Katie said. She stood up. "It was good to see you."

"Likewise," her father said.

She felt a rush of relief that the brief coffee meeting had been without conflict and had ended cordially.

It was time to head into town, but it was true that she wasn't going for the walk. She was going to see if she could find someone - or else find out more about him. His name was Gabriel Rath, and he was the person she suspected of having taken Josie.

Katie's main reason for coming here had been to try and track him down.

CHAPTER TWO

Katie left her parents' house closing the door softly behind her. But she didn't go straight into town. Instead, she walked a route that she'd never taken since the day Josie had disappeared. Now she felt compelled to revisit it. She wanted the memories to resurge, painful as she knew they would be. She needed them.

Never again, until now, had Katie followed the winding trail that led from her parents' house, through a knot of forest, and then onto the shores of the river where she'd chosen to kayak on that fateful day.

She'd thought she would be able to handle it, but as she walked, flashes of that fateful day began to surge. Tears welled in her eyes and she brushed them away with the back of her hand.

She'd been laughing with Josie, shouting down her twin's complaints, easily carrying the small kayak on her shoulder, excited about tackling the rapids. A wave of guilt washed over Katie, even now.

Laughter seemed to echo in the trees as Katie strode along. A cold drizzle began to fall, making the wooded trail even gloomier.

She'd sworn she would be responsible.

She'd lied. She'd failed.

Katie's heart was pounding. She knew she had to calm herself. That was a long time ago. She couldn't change the past.

She kept going until she came to the small clearing beside the river where she and Josie had embarked on the trip. She'd been so pleased, so excited, so sure of herself and her ability to manage the kayak. It had been a dare, a thrill, something she thought they would laugh about afterward.

She'd been wrong. And Josie had paid the price.

Gasping with unexpected, harsh sobs, Katie stared around. Everything looked just as it had on the day she'd come here with Josie.

The trees. The grass. The water.

It was as if that long ago day felt superimposed on this one. So little had changed in this timeless, rural landscape.

Katie's throat was tight with emotion. Reality was more powerful than memory. It was hard to believe this scene was the place where she had last seen her sister alive.

She had a feeling that Josie was here with her, urging her to go on.

Katie took a step forward.

The grass was wet, and she sank into the ground, nearly stumbling. She steadied herself and took another step.

She could hear the water, flowing over rocks. It was an ominous, solemn sight. The river was dark, churning, angry with the rains.

Katie shivered.

It was so different from the clear, sparkling water of summer. It looked threatening, and dangerous. It was just as it had been that day.

She walked all the way to the water's edge. She stared out at the choppy, surging water, picking up the dark rocks in the middle of the river that waited, cruel and half-hidden traps, and she shuddered.

And at that moment, memory flared, so sudden and shocking she gasped.

She'd seen him here!

She had seen him, without a doubt. In the tumult of what had happened afterward, that fleeting glimpse had been suppressed, wiped from her mind by trauma.

But now, Katie remembered.

She recalled how she'd lowered the kayak into the water, waiting for Josie to do the same. As she waited, she'd glanced at the opposite bank.

And she'd seen him. A strange, dark-clad figure, with his heavy beard and bushy hair. He'd been on the edge of the lake, holding a fishing rod, as she'd seen him do a few times in the past.

But now, on that day, Katie realized how significant his presence there had been.

He'd glanced up as the two of them set off. He'd watched them leave.

Gabriel Rath had been there! Katie breathed in a shocked gasp. Her knees felt wobbly as she took in this impossible fact.

If only she'd remembered earlier! Why had her mind repressed this critical information? Immersed in a world of trauma and pain, she'd never dared to go back to the river. She hadn't put herself in the situation where this memory would be triggered.

It matched up perfectly with what Charles Everton, the convicted serial killer, had told her in prison. He'd said he'd seen Josie, unconscious by the river bank, and he'd seen the man that Katie had later realized was Rath, taking her away.

Now, with her shock ebbing, Katie felt it replaced by a steely resolve.

She was going to hunt down Gabriel Rath, she was going to find him, and she was going to demand the truth.

What would happen after that?

Katie didn't dare think about her capacity for revenge, if he confessed to having taken her twin.

*

Ten minutes later, Katie walked into the small lakeside town, a couple of miles from her parents' house, passing the kindergarten school on the right hand side, with its colorful fence, that she'd always felt marked the start of town itself.

This was where she'd walked so many times as a child.

Her parents had believed in the small town, that it was safe for a young girl to go to the shops and back alone, that the community would look out for each other.

Now, with a sense of inevitability, Katie realized that this thinking was not in fact correct.

Her first stop was the general store. This was the hub for the community. Everyone came to the store, which sold everything from perishable foods to preserved foods to local produce, as well as basic groceries and clothing.

She swung open the door and the old-fashioned bell above it rang. This store smelled exactly the same as always, of wood and leather and a faint hint of spice. She'd forgotten the smell. Now, gooseflesh prickled her arms as she breathed it in.

The clerk behind the counter was familiar to her, too. Mrs. Mason must be in her mid-sixties now, Katie guessed, round-faced and gray-haired.

Her eyes widened in surprise.

"Well, if it isn't - Katie? Katie Winter!"

"That's right," Katie acknowledged.

"Now, this is a surprise. Years, it's been." Concern filled her kindly face as she remembered the circumstances behind Katie's move away from the community. "How are you, honey? You're looking well. Are you here seeing your parents? They were in here yesterday."

"Yes, I stopped by for a visit."

Feeling she should take a gift back to her parents, Katie took a jar of candied fruit from the shelf and handed it to her to ring up.

"That'll be six dollars, please," she smiled.

Katie paid, and as she did, she asked. "I was following up on someone in town. Trying to do some research on the past," she said.

Mrs. Mason nodded meaningfully, clearly knowing what Katie meant.

"A man called Gabriel Rath. Do you remember him?"

"Mr. Rath." A frown creased Mrs. Mason's brow. "Yes, I remember him. He used to rent one of the one-bedroom cottages. You know, down the bottom of town, those Tudor style small homes with the view of the lake?"

"Yes, I remember those."

"They were all bought up by a leisure resort a few years ago and they're now vacation rentals," Mrs. Mason continued, putting the jar in a paper bag.

"Where did Mr. Rath go?" Katie asked.

Mrs. Mason shook her head.

"I don't know where he went. You know, I don't recall seeing him for years. So many of the town came in here after - after that terrible incident with Josie. Everyone talking about it, discussing theories, wondering what they could do to help, how they could show support for your parents. But I don't recall him coming in at all now. Isn't that strange? And he always used to buy tobacco and canned food and supplies."

Katie felt more shivers prickling her back. Finally and far too late, things were adding up.

"Check next door. The bar. He was a regular there, too, and friendly with Brian, the barman. Perhaps they will know," Mrs. Mason advised.

With a cold feeling in her stomach, Katie headed next door to the bar.

She was startled to see a young, fit looking man busy opening up. This must be Brian's son. She didn't remember his name, though his shock of blonde hair was familiar. He'd only been about nine or ten when she'd left.

Now, he gave her a puzzled smile as she approached.

"Morning. We open in half an hour, or can I help some other way?" he asked.

"Your dad. Is he inside?"

"Sure. He's around the back, checking the stock. You can go in if you want to speak to him."

Katie headed into the dimly lit bar, breathing in the smell of beer and wood smoke from the enormous fireplace. She went to the back of the counter and through the door beyond.

There was Brian, a big, strong man, his blonde hair now graying.

"Hey, good morning, ma'am. Wait, I know you!" he said, turning.

"Katie Winter," she reintroduced herself.

"Katie! Good to see you back."

"I'm on a quick visit and looking for a favor," she said.

"Anything you want, I'll try to help," he promised.

"Gabriel Rath. Do you remember him? Do you know where he went? I understand he left town?"

Brian thought, frowning.

"So he did. And I don't know where he went. He was a regular here, you know. He'd come in most nights for a couple of drinks. And then, he just didn't come in anymore. I wondered about it for a month or two, and then I stopped by his rental house one day, and saw it was empty. He was gone. I mean, he must have moved out. Cleared his things. He hadn't just disappeared. So I can't tell you. Every so often, I wonder myself. But it was years ago, now. Many years." He shrugged apologetically.

"Thank you," Katie said.

She felt frustrated that her efforts were stonewalled, but more and more sure that Gabriel Rath had been involved in Josie's disappearance.

He'd taken her. And then, he'd vanished.

"Now that I think about it, there is one person who might know," Brian said.

"Who's that?" Katie asked.

"Mrs. Ingham. She used to own the cottages where he lived. She used to collect the rent in arrears and we always joked that Mrs. Ingham could follow you to your grave. I can find out where she's living now, if you like. She moved away from town, and she's staying with friends somewhere out of town. But she does come in occasionally."

"Do you know which friends?" Katie wondered if it would be easier to contact her directly.

"I have no idea. Her extended family lives off the grid now." He shrugged apologetically.

That meant she would have to wait. There was going to be no quick or easy way.

"Please ask her. Here's my card."

"I'll do what I can," he promised.

Katie handed the card over and walked out.

This had been a flying visit and she had to get back to the airport. Work had been very busy and coming here took time she didn't have available. Her job, her career, had to come first, as a priority.

She headed back out of town, feeling determined. She was not going to give up. She was going to hunt down every possible lead. She would find out what happened.

Mrs. Ingham would know something more. She felt sure of it.

CHAPTER THREE

Leblanc was out on his balcony, enjoying a late morning cup of coffee while he caught up on the paperwork from a recent case, when his phone rang.

He grabbed it up, expecting that it would either be Katie Winter, his case partner, or Detective Scott, his boss at the cross-border task force.

He felt a twist of his stomach when he saw Scott's name on the screen.

Recently, Leblanc had overheard a troubling phone conversation as he'd passed by Scott's office. From the one-sided snippets he'd picked up, Leblanc had learned that their investigation unit was under scrutiny. Something was amiss – though what, he wasn't sure.

Feeling bad about overhearing what had been a private conversation, he hadn't asked Scott about it. But in the back of his mind, he felt anxious. He felt this was a developing situation which might come to nothing, but might also end up exploding into trouble. He hoped it would just blow over, but wondered if he should share his fears with Katie when the time felt right.

"Detective Scott," he answered nervously, staring out over the St. Mary's River, which looked gray and cool on this overcast March day, winding through the scenic town of Sault Ste Marie.

"Leblanc. We have been asked by the premier of Manitoba to investigate a rather troubling set of circumstances."

He got to his feet, excitement surging. This was not about trouble for the unit, but a new case.

"What are the details?" he asked.

"A woman in her mid-twenties was found on the number 10 highway, about three hours north of Winnipeg. A local picked her up after he saw her collapsed near the road, but she seems to have come from out of the forest. She's suffering from severe exposure, and is in critical condition."

"Any idea what happened to her?" Leblanc asked.

"She has serious injuries and lacerations to her wrists and hands which the doctors have said indicate she was either bound or else got hurt trying to escape from somewhere. She's bruised on one side, indicating she might have fallen hard. She lapsed in and out of consciousness while they waited for a helicopter, and she said that she'd been abducted by a man who had told her he'd killed before."

Leblanc nodded, frowning. The scenario sent a chill down his spine. He could imagine the scene.

Spring would not yet have come to the far north of that province. A woman in the cold, terrified and injured, made his investigator's blood race.

"The victim told the driver she was from Minnesota. At least, he thinks that is what she was trying to say. He thought, from her accent, she was from the U.S. We're combing the area to see if we can pick up any additional ID for her. We've got a tracker dog on the scene. But if she is in fact an American citizen, this puts the incident firmly into our jurisdiction."

"Understood," Leblanc agreed.

"Even if she isn't, the premier of Manitoba has asked us to investigate, as it's extremely troubling and doesn't appear to be a typical domestic violence incident."

"Agreed. That's not typical and, especially if she's from Minnesota, there might be more to it," Leblanc said.

"They are extremely short of manpower in the province, especially in this season, and policing is thinly stretched. This incident is disturbing. He's extremely worried that it will explode once the media latch onto it, and that it will affect tourism in the province with spring just a month away. He wants us to look into it and see if we can figure out the circumstances behind it, what really happened, and who was responsible."

"The media is a big concern, and I agree it needs to be looked into," Leblanc agreed.

"Will you get ahold of Katie? I know she's on her way back from New York state this morning," Scott continued.

"I will," Leblanc confirmed.

"You two can fly straight out to Winnipeg. I'll organize with the local RCMP to take it from there. There aren't many details so far but it's a developing case. I'll send you updates as they arrive, as well as your travel arrangements, if you can get to the airport."

"I'll get there right away," he confirmed, and ended the call.

Leblanc felt excited to be on a new case, as he headed inside to add a few items to the travel bag he kept packed. Putting his laptop and phone inside, he was ready to go.

He grabbed his bag and headed for the door, picking up the keys to his car. As soon as he was in the car, he called Katie.

She answered, sounding as if she was walking fast.

"Hey there," he said, feeling a smile warm his face.

Upon hearing her voice, he felt totally at peace with the decision he'd recently made to turn his back forever on his past.

Leblanc knew both he and Katie were scarred by what they'd had to live through.

Leblanc had spent years working as an investigator in Paris. But the shocking murder of Celeste, his investigation partner and lover, had almost derailed Leblanc and forced him into a series of life changes. Guilt had corroded him after she was killed by a convict during a prison riot. He knew things could have been different if he had only been there with her at the time.

The thoughts of revenge that had clouded his mind had nearly forced him into a series of disastrous decisions. But now, thanks mainly to Katie's intervention, he'd put that aside. Leblanc was no longer interested in retribution. He wanted to move forward, embrace his new career with the cross-border task force, and put all his energies into the future.

Even in the short time since he'd made this decision, he felt liberated. He felt as if he could breathe again; and in the work he was doing, he felt more useful than he'd ever felt before.

The only small complication was that he knew he was starting to become deeply involved with Katie Winter. Emotionally, she was more than just a colleague. Physically, he desired her.

He was falling in love with her.

Leblanc knew he was getting in deep, and that it was serious. And yet, he was powerless to do anything other than follow this path.

And he wanted to, but he also knew that it could be dangerous to do so.

He couldn't bear to lose another partner, which brought a level of complexity to their relationship. He knew he already cared for her deeply.

But their job was filled with risk, and that was a fact.

"Hey Leblanc," she replied. "I'm heading for the airplane on the last leg of the journey home."

He knew she'd been visiting her family. It sounded as if things hadn't gone badly. Perhaps they'd gone well. He knew she was also hopeful to discover more about her twin's disappearance, but there wasn't time to speak about that now.

"We have a new case," he confirmed.

"We do? Where?" He heard the same tension in her voice, now.

"It's in Manitoba. Scott is booking us on a flight to Winnipeg. So when you land at Sault Ste Marie, I'll meet you at the airport and we can go straight from there."

"Sounds good," Katie said. "I can't wait to hear more."

"I'll send you the details as soon as Scott sends them to me." He cut the call and focused on the road ahead.

Although, in Sault Ste Marie, there were faint signs of spring - emergence of grass, a warming of the weather, and a few frost-free days - he knew that the more northerly part of Manitoba was at least a month behind in terms of weather.

Spring would bring new opportunities for tourism in a province that had much to offer visitors, and which Leblanc personally loved. He'd always thought of Manitoba as one of the most peaceful places, and the taint of a crime like this could have far reaching consequences.

Leblanc realized that the premier was being very cautious in calling them out at such an early stage, but he appreciated that he was thinking ahead and looking to get answers before fear erupted and difficult questions were asked.

In the northern regions, with their vast distances and small populations, a killer could easily move undetected, evading capture and hiding from law enforcement.

It would take specialized knowledge and skill to track down this individual and Leblanc was fully on board with starting sooner. This was a puzzling case with a scarcity of information. Who had abducted this girl; how had she ended up suffering from exposure and stumbling out of a snowbound forest? What were the circumstances behind it, and would she ever recover enough to be able to explain more about her ordeal? Leblanc knew that exposure could cause serious and lasting damage. Just because the young woman was in the hospital did not yet mean she was out of danger, or even that she would recover.

Leblanc knew this was going to be a challenge, and he hoped that between him and Katie, they could get to the truth of what had happened and find the evil person who was responsible for her plight.

CHAPTER FOUR

Katie sat next to Leblanc on the airplane headed to Winnipeg. She felt intrigued by this new case, disturbing as it was. She looked forward to immersing herself in the challenge of piecing together what had happened.

Going home, and focusing on her twin's disappearance, always opened old wounds. Having something else to set her mind to, helped to ease the pain. It also gave her a sense of purpose, that even though she might never solve her sister's cold case, she could pour all her energies into solving others.

As she glanced out of the airplane window, she wondered about their new case.

First of all, the terrain and climate in the more northern regions of Manitoba were incredibly harsh. She knew that the long, cold winters and snow-covered terrain made this a tough environment.

The area was vast, and sparsely populated, with a huge amount of wilderness. This meant that the task of fighting crime was difficult and time consuming. It was also a major logistical headache.

She would not be surprised if this woman's captor had, in fact, killed before. It was entirely possible that he'd told her the truth, or that she'd learned it for herself. And there was no other logical cause for those type of injuries. Nor for the fact she'd been found after an extended period outside at night, inadequately dressed for the weather, and in the middle of nowhere.

Given that the report had mentioned no dwellings or settlements in the area, Katie wondered if she'd managed to struggle free while being transported somewhere in a car, van, truck, or other vehicle. Falling out of a moving car could have accounted for the scrapes and bruises. Perhaps she'd fled, hoping that her captor would not follow, but had then gotten lost in the forest and taken hours to find her way back to the road.

Already, this case was preoccupying all her thoughts as she tried to puzzle out what could have happened.

Leblanc, too, was engrossed in the case file.

"The victim said she was from Minnesota, but the driver who found her is not totally sure about that as she was very incoherent. Nobody is yet sure where or why she ended up in the middle of nowhere, or why she was in the woods," he said. "They've got a dog following her tracks and are looking for any more information on who she is and where she came from."

"Could she have been abducted? Held captive somewhere and then moved? I hope they get an ID soon, and that her family can provide more information," Katie said.

"She was found hypothermic and frostbitten, ranting and raving about a man who had said he was going to kill her, and said he had killed before." Leaning over his shoulder, Katie read on.

"She was in a state of terror and had lacerations on her hands and wrists."

She shook her head. This was triggering. She imagined Josie all over again. Josie had been taken. What had she felt? Had she been left alive or tried to get away?

"She must have been trapped inside somewhere, or tied up somehow. How did she get those lacerations? Trying to free herself?" Katie theorized.

"Our first stop needs to be the hospital," Leblanc said.

Katie nodded. "I hope we can get something coherent from her. It sounds as if she was in critical condition."

He nodded somberly.

The plane was coming in to land, and Katie glanced down at the aerial view of Winnipeg.

"I've never been to Winnipeg before," she said, thinking that the treed view, although icy, looked scenic. She guessed it would be a pleasant place to live.

"I have been here before," Leblanc admitted. "I like the city. I find it a relaxed place. More like a big town, in its feel and character."

Katie kept looking out of the window as the plane descended, taking in the details and character of this serene city.

They touched down, and she dragged her attention away from the view. There was work to be done and a criminal to hunt down.

As the plane came to a stop, she grabbed her bag and her coat. Walking toward the door, she felt the heat of the plane quickly replaced by the frigid air of outside.

The small airport was buzzing, a hive of activity. With no checked-in luggage, they headed quickly through. As soon as they walked into the arrival hall, she spotted the person they were looking for. He was an RCMP officer, holding a sign with their names on. He was a tall man, wearing a thick parka, with a broad, pleasant face.

They headed over to him.

"Good morning," he said. "I'm Officer Lance Muldoon. I'm part of the local team who has been assigned this case."

"Good to meet you," Katie said. "We'd like to go straight to the hospital and interview the witness."

"Yes. I'm going to take you there as a priority. Come this way."

Quickly, he wove his way through the airport and out to where an RCMP vehicle was stopped outside the building.

A few minutes later, they were driving away from the airport, and toward the hospital.

Katie looked around, taking in the sights and the senses of Winnipeg. Under a cold blue sky, the city looked clean and pristine. She was interested in the combination of architecture she saw as they drove, from stately high-rises, to Beaux-Art and Chicago-style warehouses and buildings. She agreed with Leblanc and thought it looked like a pleasant, peaceful place to live.

It was not a place where you expected a shocking crime like an abduction to occur, but Katie knew only too well that evil could lurk anywhere.

Even in the most innocent riverside town, where two teenagers were setting off on a kayaking dare, believing that the worst that could happen was an unexpected dunking in the water.

Officer Muldoon stopped his vehicle at the hospital's front entrance, parking in an emergency bay.

"I'll come in with you, and take you straight to her ward."

They walked into the hospital.

Muldoon detoured to the front desk, muttering a quick explanation to the receptionist, while Katie breathed in the smell of disinfectant, taking in the neat, austere surroundings of this small but busy hospital.

"Right. We have permission to go to her ward. She's in high care but might be moved to ICU at any moment. The doctor in charge is willing to let you speak to her briefly, but only one of you may go in."

Leblanc glanced at Katie.

"You go," he said. "I'll wait here."

Katie nodded, feeling thankful that Leblanc wanted her to go in. Difficult as seeing this critically ill woman was going to be, she wanted to see the victim for herself, and hoped that she would be able to pick up anything she had to say.

"She's on the second floor," Muldoon said, walking to the elevator with Katie following.

"Has she been able to speak further about what happened?" Katie asked, as they walked along the quiet corridors.

"I believe not. They had her deeply sedated at first. They're bringing her out of it now to see how she responds."

Katie walked down the corridor to the high care ward, treading over the polished tiles, hoping that she would get lucky, and that this young woman would be coherent. She knew that the next few minutes would be vital. She had to make the most of them.

Ahead, she saw a nurse's station at the entrance to the high care ward. A nursing sister stepped forward to meet them.

"This is the FBI agent who would like to ask the patient some questions," Muldoon explained.

The nurse nodded. She was a serious looking, dark-haired woman in her forties. She turned to Katie.

"I'm Nurse Harte, the sister in charge of this ward. You may spend a few minutes with the patient. She's in a ward on her own."

"Thank you," Katie said.

"I must reiterate that she is in a very serious condition. She's still lightly sedated. We may have to put her on life support at any moment. I can allow you only a couple of minutes with her. Her own life and health comes first." She stared firmly at Katie.

Katie nodded, understanding the seriousness, but glad to have the permission to try. Whatever this young woman could tell them would be helpful, but she sensed that the nurse was not sure she was in a state to offer any helpful information.

Katie could only hope that luck and timing would allow her to communicate with this desperately ill patient.

Nurse Harte led Katie down the corridor, and then paused outside a closed door.

"This is the ward," she said, quietly.

Katie glanced up and down the corridor, hoping that this unknown patient would have recovered enough to explain what had happened. There was no certainty of that. Her condition was serious. She might never be able to describe what had played out, but Katie had to try.

She took a deep breath, then pushed the door. It swung open, and she stepped inside.

CHAPTER FIVE

The quiet beeping of machines seemed to fill the small, warm room as Katie paced across the floor to the bed.

She stared down, feeling a pang of regret at what she saw.

A young woman, in the prime of her life, now lying on a hospital bed. Her face was so pale it almost seemed bruised.

Nurse Harte trod behind her, a silent, watchful presence, and Katie knew that her first priority would be the well-being of her patient.

The hot air smelled faintly sickly to her, and her stomach twisted.

The woman looked small and fragile as she lay motionless on the bed. She was breathing shallowly, and did not stir. She was hooked up to monitors, and her vitals were flashing up on the screens behind her.

Her right arm was bruised, as if she had been in a fight. That must have been from a fall, surely, Katie guessed, taking in the skinned elbow. Her lips were chapped and bleeding, which must be from the cold. Her yellow-blonde hair was at odds with the pale white of her face. Katie could see bandages on her wrists and hands from the deeper lacerations.

She wished she knew her name. Speaking it might create recognition and help pull her out of this twilight zone where she was lingering.

All she could do was say, by way of introduction, "I hope you are feeling better soon. I'm Katie Winter."

The woman didn't stir. Her eyes were closed.

Katie moved closer to the bed, and spoke again.

"It's okay. I'm from the police. We are trying to help you," Katie said. "We need to find the person responsible for this. I know that you've been through an ordeal. Can you tell us what happened to you?"

But only silence greeted her.

"Can you hear me?" Katie asked.

She waited for a moment, and then there was a flicker of a response. Her eyes fluttered, and she let out a soft moan.

"It's okay," she said again, a little louder. This time, the patient's eyes opened. Katie felt a rush of encouragement. Perhaps she might be able to talk.

"Do you remember what happened to you?" Katie asked.

She was trying to keep her voice level and soothing, focusing on the young woman. Her lips moved. A soundless word. Katie bent forward.

Her lips were fluttering. She was trying to speak.

To her frustration, Katie couldn't make out the word clearly. Was it 'Driver'? She thought perhaps that was what she was trying to say.

She felt weirdly close to this young woman, but at the same time too far away, separated by the sedation and confusion, the critical state of her health, that did not allow her to communicate what had happened.

Katie knew that, important as it was to get information, she could not do it at the patient's cost. She had a feeling that her time here was about to be cut short.

Nurse Harte was now standing beside her, monitoring the patient, as well as the information on the screens.

"I'm sorry, agent," she said, her voice anxious. "Her vitals are not looking good, and we're going to have to sedate her again. I think it's time to put her on life support. I'm going to have to ask you to leave."

Katie turned quickly away. "Thank you," she said softly.

She hurried out of the ward, hoping that this desperately ill woman would recover from her terrible ordeal.

Heading downstairs again, she saw that Leblanc was standing near the exit door with officer Muldoon.

She hurried over to him.

"I didn't get much," she said regretfully. "She's in a very serious condition. I got one word, which was 'Driver', I think. But that's not a lot to go on. I was hoping she'd be more coherent. I just hope she survives."

Leblanc nodded.

"We have another possible lead," he said. "The motorist who found her lives here in Winnipeg. He's a local who was returning from an ice fishing trip up north. We can go and speak to him now. He's already been interviewed by the police, but he might have recalled something more, as he was a state of anxiety when he found her. He's at home now. Muldoon has just confirmed."

"That sounds promising," Katie agreed.

Speaking to the man who had picked up this woman might give them more valuable information.

They followed Muldoon out of the hospital, and again Katie shivered, realizing how warm it had been in there, and how icy it still was outside. They hustled back to the car and climbed inside.

"This witness's name is David Sommers. He lives on College Avenue," Muldoon said. "It's just a short drive from here."

He started the car and pulled away from the hospital, heading toward the outskirts of town.

As they drove, Katie was quiet, still processing the sight of that frail woman in the hospital bed. It had shocked her deeply. She hoped David Sommers would have remembered some important facts.

In another minute, Muldoon pulled the car up outside a small house built of dark wood, with a red painted front door. It was set in a small but tidy yard, with conifers flanking the home. Behind it, Katie saw a backdrop of snow covered hills and forest.

They climbed out and headed up to the front door, with Katie's breath misting in the air.

She knocked, and David Sommers opened it almost immediately.

He was a man who looked to be in his fifties, with a long, brown beard, and kind looking eyes. He was wearing a thick, navy blue sweater and jeans.

"Agent Winter and Detective Leblanc," Katie introduced them.

"Oh, I'm glad you're here," he said. "Please, come in."

He led them to a small dining room where they took seats around the circular table. On the walls were framed prints of landscapes – deep forests, blue lakes. Clearly, Sommers was a lover of nature.

"Coffee?" he asked, quickly pouring from a tray he had ready.

"Can you tell me more about how and when you found the victim?" Katie asked, accepting the coffee gratefully.

"I was driving back from my fishing trip with three friends, very early this morning. I had to be back home by eight for a work meeting. I canceled it after what happened," he explained. "Anyway, I had spent a couple of days at a campsite about four hours north of here, on highway 10. My friends were staying another day, but I packed up my gear and got on the road by four-thirty a.m. I'd driven for an hour or so, in the pitch dark, when I saw her running onto the road. She was stumbling, looking like she was about to collapse. It gave me a massive shock. I didn't know what had happened."

Katie could see the trauma in his eyes.

"She was clearly in a very bad way. There was nobody else on the road. I got her into the car immediately and turned up the heater. I tried to find out what had happened."

"Was she able to speak?" Katie asked.

"She was sort of incoherent. She was shaking terribly. Her hands and wrists were covered in dried blood. I put my jacket around her and tried to get her as warm as possible. I then called the emergency services. They said they'd send a helicopter out, and that I must just keep her as warm as possible in the car. So I did that. The helicopter took about half an hour to get here, distances being what they are."

He shook his head. Katie could see the episode had been traumatic for him.

"Did she talk at all?" he asked.

"Yes. She talked, but a lot of it didn't make sense. I wish now I'd recorded it or something. I remember her saying she'd been trapped, that someone had held her prisoner and she was going to be killed. She said he'd told her he'd killed before. And to me, she definitely sounded American. Not local. I asked her where she was from and she said Minnesota. I asked her name, but that was one of the questions she didn't seem to hear."

"It sounds like that must have been an ordeal for you, too," Katie sympathized.

"I feel like a wreck," David explained. "I was starting to feel really jumpy and afraid in that car. I was expecting someone to come after her at any moment. And I was so worried for her own welfare. I mean, I was thinking she could die at any moment. She looked terribly cold and ill."

"Did she give a timeframe? How long she'd been trapped? When she'd escaped?"

"No, not at all," David said. "That's all I can remember."

Katie exchanged a quick glance with Leblanc. She thought they were done here. This information had confirmed that the girl had perceived herself to be in serious danger and that she'd clearly believed she was in the hands of a killer. Given the injuries and what she'd gone through, Katie accepted it.

She finished her coffee.

"If you remember anything else, please call," she said.

"I will do," David promised.

As they headed out, Muldoon's phone beeped.

"There's been some progress," he said. "The search team just updated me. They've gotten an ID on the victim. The sniffer dog found a jacket in the woods with an ID in the pocket. Name of Sherrie Blair, from Minneapolis, Minnesota. I don't know why it would have been there or how she lost it."

"In advanced hypothermia, she might have removed it. In that delirious state, a person can sometimes feel as if they are too hot, rather than too cold," Katie remembered.

"That would account for it. Anyway, the dog found nothing further, and no other scents nearby. Mrs. Blair has been notified, and is already on a plane to Winnipeg. She'll land in about half an hour. I'm sure she'll be anxious to go to her daughter immediately, but we could probably speak to her at the airport first."

CHAPTER SIX

Katie waited in the arrival hall, feeling hopeful that this might lead to a breakthrough in the case. Perhaps Sherrie might have shared information with her mother. Mrs. Blair might know more about her movements prior to her abduction.

It was a deeply troubling situation and, standing in the drafty hall, Katie turned the information over and over in her mind.

Why had Sherrie whispered that word 'Driver'? What did she mean by it? Did the driver who had found her know more? Had she hitched a ride with a car or truck, and was she referring to that person?

And why had she stumbled alone out of the woods? Had someone been searching for her, chasing her? Had she managed to lose them in the icy woods, or had David's arrival on the scene scared them off? There were so many unknowns. She shivered, and not just from the chill in the air.

Muldoon was waiting with them, in uniform, and holding a notice with Mrs. Blair's name on it. He'd arranged to meet Mrs. Blair and drop her off at the hospital so she could immediately be with her daughter.

Katie's thoughts were with the mother. She could only imagine how she must feel, having just received such a bombshell about her critically ill daughter. She must be totally traumatized. This was not going to be an easy time for her and she deeply sympathized with her plight.

The flight had landed. Passengers were beginning to filter through and Katie watched to see who would see the sign and head their way.

She spotted Mrs. Blair straight away, because she was looking tearful and stressed as she headed through the gates. An attractive woman in her early fifties, she had thick blonde hair, and was dressed in a stylish navy blue outfit that made Katie think she'd probably flown here straight from work.

"Mrs. Blair?" she said, as the woman walked up to them.

"Yes, I'm Sherrie's mother," she replied breathlessly. "I seriously can't believe this. I feel like I'm in a nightmare. My daughter! If only I could turn back time."

She drew a Kleenex from a purse that looked crammed with them, and dabbed her eyes.

"We're going to take you straight to the hospital," Muldoon reassured her. "This case is a top priority, which is why we've got these two members of the special investigation unit assisting us. Agent Winter would like to ask you some questions on the way, so that we can try to piece together more about Sherrie's circumstances without taking up too much of your time."

"Sure. Sure."

She'd come with no luggage. Only her purse. Katie decided to wait until they were in the car before asking anything further. They walked in silence through the airport, and headed out to the police cruiser.

Muldoon opened the door for Mrs. Blair. She climbed into the back, and Katie got in next to her. Leblanc took the passenger seat in front.

"I'm so sorry about your daughter. You must be beside yourself with worry," Katie said sympathetically. "For now, though, it will help us so much to know more about the background. Do you know when she arrived in Canada, where she went, why she traveled here?"

Katie waiting for her to gather herself together. She could imagine how many emotions were warring in the poor woman's mind. She felt desperately sorry for her.

"She traveled here to be with a boyfriend who lives further north," Mrs. Blair said. "In a town called The Pas. They met when he was vacationing near where we live in Minneapolis."

"What's his name?" Katie asked.

"His name is Benjamin Stratton," she said. "He works in a paper mill. He's about thirty years old, and I didn't approve of this at all." Now Katie could see how traumatized she looked.

"I'm sorry," she said, as Mrs. Blair took another Kleenex out of her purse and wiped her eyes.

"I was very against her going to see him. It sounded like he was asking her to move in with him permanently; that was what I picked up. She was twenty-two! She's just finished at the university! She's been studying to be an archaeologist, like her father. We never had much money, and she's worked so hard to get her degree. I felt like by coming here, she was throwing it all away on a man I didn't think was suitable." She sighed.

"I understand," Katie said.

"And I didn't like him as a person. So I cut her off financially. I said if she goes, I'm not supporting her. I was so angry. No wonder she didn't get in touch with me again."

Clearly, the mother's decisions and Sherrie's actions had caused fault lines within their relationship to develop and widen. Katie was reminded painfully of how her own family had also cracked and broken in a pressured situation.

"How long had she known him?"

"Only a couple of months."

"And how long had she stayed there with him?"

"She left to go and be with him about two weeks ago. I told her we were no longer going to communicate with her if she did that, and she wasn't to ask for any money or any help. We had a big fight the day she left." She blew her nose and took a deep breath. "I will never forgive myself. I think she must have been trying to get back home. I just have no idea what could have happened."

"Did she communicate with you at all?"

"She sent me a text to say she'd arrived, and a photo of the view. I didn't reply. I still felt so hurt and angry. She was the one who tried to reach out and mend things. I was the one who refused to do the same."

Katie saw Leblanc nodding, taking in the pain of the situation that had gone bad beyond anyone's imagining.

Mrs. Blair continued. "If I'd been more reasonable, if I'd stayed in touch with her, I could have understood what was going on. I don't know what happened! Did she leave him and meet up with someone else? Did he do this to her? I just have no idea what could have played out."

"Please, don't blame yourself," Katie pleaded. "Nobody could have known this would happen."

"As a parent, I should never have put my child in a situation where it could happen," she insisted tearfully.

"Why didn't you like Benjamin?" Katie asked, hoping to get more perspective on him. "Can you tell us about her relationship with this boyfriend?" She needed some information on the dynamic between them, and whether he could have been involved in this crime.

"He was way too keen to rush into a commitment with her. I mean, they'd known each other only a few weeks and it was mostly a long distance relationship, but then he started pressuring her to marry him. He wanted her to go and live with him. He wanted her to give up what she had back home. I started to worry he thought of her as a convenient little wife that he could take back to The Pas to care for him."

She shrugged miserably.

"And how did you feel about him as a person?" Katie asked.

"I suspected he was the kind of person who could be abusive, just because he came across as rather controlling. I didn't like him at all. Perhaps I got the wrong impression, but I felt he was, like, a typical domineering man who just expects that a woman will be secondary to him. But now I don't know what she found out when she went there. She could have had to endure a terrible time. All on her own, with her mother not speaking to her. I might never know now."

Her voice sounded full of despair. "I should have known something was wrong. I should have realized."

"Would she have stayed in touch with any other friends?" Katie asked.

"I don't know what her situation was. If she was out of money, she might not have been able to communicate. And maybe he didn't want her venting to her friends. Like I said, he had controlling tendencies. I wish I'd helped her."

Katie shook her head, feeling sympathetic for the mother's predicament, but acknowledging inwardly that if the lines of communication had stayed open, her daughter could have been alive and well.

She wondered briefly whether, if her own parents' reaction had been different, she would have remembered more about Gabriel Rath earlier. The rejection, the blame, had all sealed the memories deep inside at that traumatic time.

"Anything else that you can think of, any other information or small details, which might help us?" Katie asked.

Mrs. Blair frowned, thinking.

"I would have thought Sherrie was too smart to get into trouble; she was always so bright and capable," she said. "She loved her archaeology. She wanted to discover new things. She had an incredible interest in the world. She was always going to be an adventurer." She looked at Katie with tears flowing again. "I thought if she went to Manitoba, she'd fall right into the hands of that man."

"We're almost at the hospital," Muldoon said from the driver's seat.

Turning away from Katie, Mrs. Blair glanced anxiously out of the window.

Katie didn't want to delay her a moment.

"Thank you for your time," she said, as Muldoon pulled up outside the hospital.

Mrs. Blair scrambled out and rushed inside. Watching her, Katie felt sad and worried. Sherrie had not looked in a good way at all. She feared that this mother might never speak to her child again.

But as difficult as this interview had been, they now had an important piece of information.

There had been a boyfriend in the picture, who might have been abusive and controlling. Sherrie had been involved in a potentially volatile relationship. Something must have gone wrong, and even if Benjamin had not been a part of it, he could know more.

"Muldoon, is there a possibility of getting a helicopter up to The Pas?" she asked. "It's probably a six hour drive up there, and we don't have the time for that. We need to talk to Benjamin urgently," Katie said.

"Agreed," Muldoon said. "I'll organize it now. I hope you can find out what happened after her daughter left. From what this mother said, it could be this boyfriend was involved, or knows who took her."

CHAPTER SEVEN

Leblanc checked his watch as the helicopter came in to land. He'd never been to The Pas before. From the air, he thought the town looked attractive. A winding river - the Saskatchewan River - bisected it, and the town itself was set among treed wilderness that, in mid-March, was still icy and frozen.

He remembered that the population of this town was a little over five thousand, a sizable settlement for one that was relatively far north.

Among these five thousand, would they find the criminal here?

It would not have been possible for Sherrie Blair to have gotten all the way from this town, to where she was found, on foot. It was too great a distance, and too cold. She'd undoubtedly been taken all, or most, of the way in a vehicle of some kind. Now, they needed to try and track her movements, her interactions, to see how that had happened and who had driven her out of town.

That word 'Driver'. Hopefully it described someone they could find here.

The helicopter touched down on the helipad of the local RCMP department just outside of downtown. Leblanc thanked the pilot and climbed out, shivering as the cold hit him. He watched as Katie did the same, instinctively tugging her coat closed in the icy breeze.

Scott had messaged them to say he'd briefed the local RCMP precinct commander, who was waiting at the helipad to meet them. He was a genial, plump man with a trimmed mustache and a welcoming smile.

"I'm Officer Jim McWilliams," he said, shaking hands with Leblanc. "Welcome to The Pas. Pity about the circumstances, and I hope you can make progress with this crime."

"Thanks for meeting us," Leblanc said.

"We've made a vehicle available to you. If you need anything further, or any backup from our side, please ask us. There's a radio in the vehicle, and here's my card, and the keys," he offered.

"Thanks," Katie said, taking the card and keys from him.

Leblanc acknowledged that in the snow and ice, she was a much more capable driver than him. And although these roads had been plowed, there was no telling what might happen, or where they might end up heading.

He scrambled quickly into the passenger seat of the gray Ford in the parking lot, glad to get out of the biting wind.

He checked his iPad, looking for the details they'd obtained on Benjamin Stratton.

"He lives at number four Clover Road, and he works at the paper mill. Given that it's now three-thirty p.m. on a weekday, I'm guessing he'll be at work," Leblanc said.

"Agreed." Katie started the car. "Let's head to the paper mill and take it from there."

After programming the address into his maps, Leblanc looked out of the window as they drove, taking in the snow-covered trees, a wide expanse of white fields, and the river winding its way through town, with bridges for cars and pedestrians traversing it.

The paper mill was located on the opposite side of the river from the airport. They drove over a wide bridge, and Leblanc glanced down at the deeply frozen water below. Once across the bridge, and into the more industrial side of town, they drove another minute before arriving at the parking lot of the paper mill.

It was a vast brick building with smoke spewing from several smokestacks. It had a massive backyard and a few warehouses attached.

Katie stopped inside the paved parking lot, and they climbed out and headed to the door. Leblanc felt expectant, and hoped that Benjamin Stratton would be at work and, more importantly, would have information that could take them further.

Katie walked inside, with Leblanc following.

"Good afternoon. We're police detectives, investigating a crime," Katie introduced herself to the receptionist, who was wrapped up in a coat, hat, and gloves, and nestled next to a heater. In this vast space, Leblanc knew, manning this desk must be like working inside a freezer. "We need to speak to Benjamin Stratton urgently. Is he at work?"

"Mr. Stratton?" The receptionist checked her computer. "He's on shift at the moment. He'll have to clock out. Can you go to the waiting room, and I'll ask him to join you." She indicated a small room on the side, which Leblanc thought didn't look any warmer.

They walked in and perched on two of the plastic chairs. The environment was noisy, and the sounds reverberated in the large space. Grinding of motors, the constant hum of engines, and the rattle of machinery permeated the air.

Leblanc clasped his hands together for warmth, wishing he'd brought his gloves inside. He exchanged a brief glance with Katie, who was waiting in silence, looking preoccupied with her thoughts.

In another moment, there was a different noise - approaching footsteps.

A tall, curly-haired man who looked to be about thirty walked in. He looked nervous, and surprised to see them. He was wearing a dull green parka and a woolen hat.

"Good afternoon." Katie stood immediately. "Mr. Stratton?"

"Yes." He frowned. "What's this about? Are you sure you have the right person? I have no idea what's going on here."

"We're investigating a crime at the moment, and we need to talk to you. May we have a few moments of your time?" She gestured to the chair. "Please, have a seat."

"Yes, of course." He sat down, looking around. "What crime?"

"Do you know a woman called Sherrie Blair?" Katie continued.

Benjamin looked astounded.

"Sherrie?" he said incredulously.

"Yes. We understand she arrived here about two weeks ago, and has been staying with you."

"She did, but - hang on, a crime?" Now his voice sounded anxious. "What's happened? Has anything happened to her?"

"Yes. It appears she was abducted. She escaped, and was found early this morning, in a remote woodland bordering the number 10 highway. She's in critical condition in the hospital and we're trying to piece together what happened."

The information seemed to take a moment to sink in, and Benjamin's face blanched.

"I don't believe this. I have no idea who would do that to her." His eyes widened. "I can't actually process this. Do you think she'll be okay? What do you need to know?"

Leblanc perceived that his confusion and his shock was genuine. He guessed that Benjamin most definitely had not known about this. His reaction was exactly what Leblanc would have expected.

" We don't know yet what the prognosis is. When did you last see her?" Katie asked.

"Yesterday, after I got back from work." Now Benjamin looked horrified. "We - look, we'd been fighting. It wasn't working out. We had a huge fight when I got back from work, and she said that's it, she was leaving. I said I was going to go to gym and she should just calm down and we could talk about it later. But she said when I got back, she wouldn't be here anymore."

"Did she say how she was going to leave?" Leblanc asked, wondering how that decision had precipitated her into the situation where she'd been abducted.

"I said I wasn't going to take her anywhere, and she said I didn't have to because she was going to get a cab to the airport. I mean, it sounded final. Like she was going to fly back and I'd never see her again. I was mad at her and upset. I didn't try talk her out of it. I just said, go on then, get the hell out. And went to the gym. She wasn't home when I got back. She'd taken her bag. I didn't know what to do. I've been wondering all day what to do."

"Do you know what cab she would have called?"

"She would probably have called City Cabs. We used them and Uber while she was here, but I remember she couldn't connect to Uber from her phone here. I've no idea why, it was some kind of a software glitch I think. So I guess she would have used City Cabs."

Was this the driver they were seeking? A cab driver? Leblanc felt a flare of excitement at the possibility they had solved this puzzle.

"Anyone else she spoke to, or befriended, while she was here? Did she have any disagreements with anyone? Any causes for concern that you can remember?" Katie asked.

Benjamin shook his head.

"No, I don't think so. She kept to herself, but I think that was because she didn't know anyone, and we were going through a bad patch. And we did go out with my friends a couple of times, but the problem was I was working back to back shifts and their timing was all wrong these past weeks."

Leblanc was glad they'd asked these questions, to confirm that there was nobody else who might have had a motive for this crime.

"Can you confirm you were at the gym, and that she was gone when you got back?" Leblanc asked.

"Yes. I swiped my card at the gym, to get the fitness points. And when I got back and she wasn't there, I called my friend and asked what I should do. We ended up going out for a drink and discussing it. I didn't feel good about it. I wanted to call her immediately, but he said to wait. That she was gone and I should wait till tomorrow and think calmly."

"Okay," Leblanc said.

He was ninety percent convinced by Benjamin's version, but there were gaps in the timeline that still might have allowed for him to have committed the crime himself. He could have purposely set out to create an alibi, while planning revenge after the explosive fight.

That meant that it would now be very important to confirm whether Sherrie had used a cab. If she'd gotten into the cab, then Benjamin would be completely cleared and the focus would be on the cab driver.

Why hadn't she ended up at her destination?

It was time to get answers, from the City Cabs driver who Sherrie had trusted with the airport transfer.

CHAPTER EIGHT

As soon as they were back in the car, Katie looked up the address for City Cabs.

"I think we need to go there in person," she told Leblanc. "We're going to have questions that need more detail than an operator is going to be able to give out over the phone."

"Their address is about seven blocks from here, toward the center of town," he replied, looking it up on his phone. "Here you go. I've programmed it into maps."

"Okay. While I drive, will you call and ask to speak to the manager?"

Leblanc got on the phone immediately.

"Good morning," he said, as soon as the operator answered. "We're police investigators, following up on a crime. We'll be at your premises in five minutes and would like to have a quick interview with your manager. It's urgent."

"Sure." The woman sounded surprised. "Mr. Martins is available. I'll tell him you're on your way."

Katie glanced at the map, which was telling her that after one left turn and one right turn, they would pull up outside City Cabs.

The company was housed in a yellow-painted building that was unmistakable from a long way off. Katie wondered what the neighboring businesses had thought of that garish color choice. There were a number of cabs, and also a few private vehicles in the parking bays outside. She took the last available bay and climbed out.

Quickly, they walked inside.

Two operators wearing headsets were sitting at the reception desk, but Katie headed straight for the nervous looking man standing to their right.

"Mr. Martins?" she asked.

"That's me," he agreed. He was short and stocky looking, with neatly trimmed brown hair. He looked like a serious and methodical person. "Please, come to my office."

He led the way behind the reception desk, into a small, neat, and very warm office. He took a seat behind the desk and gestured for them to take the two other chairs.

"How can I help the police this afternoon?" he asked apprehensively.

"We're investigating a serious crime," Katie said. "A woman was abducted, and is currently in a hospital suffering from severe exposure. We're tracing her movements before the time she was taken and trying to piece together what happened."

"And you - you think our cab company was responsible?" the manager stuttered, looking appalled. "We do background checks on our drivers. We don't hire criminals or rogue individuals."

"Understood," Leblanc said firmly. He gave the manager a stern look, which silenced his protests.

I need to know which of your drivers took a customer from four Clover Road, to the airport, yesterday evening," Katie continued.

The manager frowned, as if still worried that this might bring trouble down on the company.

"Let me check," he said, turning to the laptop. He tapped a few keys and waited.

"That would have been Fred Weaver. He wasn't scheduled to work yesterday, but we called him in as a substitute. The call-out for the airport ride came in at six-forty-five p.m., I see here. But that trip was not completed."

Katie glanced at Leblanc, seeing the same surprise in his eyes.

"Why not?" she asked.

"I have no idea." The manager shook his head. "According to this log, he arrived at the address for the pickup, but then aborted the trip a short while later. We do ask for reasons, but he hasn't yet provided any."

Excitement flared within Katie. This was sounding like it might lead somewhere.

"Has Weaver been working for you for long?"

"No, not long. We hired him recently, and he still works on a part-time basis. Another full-time driver was sick so we called him in."

Katie had one more question, wanting to piece together this man's movements and whether he would have had the opportunity to drive out of town with Sherrie.

"Did he have any other bookings after that aborted trip?"

"No, he went off shift straight afterward. That's why I guess he didn't update on the reasons yet."

"And is he on duty now?" Leblanc asked.

"No."

"Could you give me the make, model, and number plate of his car, please?" Katie asked.

"Sure. I'll print that info for you. It's a tan Toyota Corolla. Last year's model. Up to spec for what we require from our drivers."

The printer whirred and he handed Katie the page.

"What's his home address, please?" Katie asked.

Looking even more worried now, he complied.

"He lives at number forty Circle Drive. I do hope this won't land our company in any trouble. Should we take any action against Mr. Weaver?"

"Sir, at the moment we are simply looking for information to take us further with the case," Katie said. "There's no reason at all for your company to be in trouble, or for Mr. Weaver to be in trouble, if he is able to answer our questions."

But despite Katie's routine reply, she felt deeply concerned at the chain of events that had played out.

"I think that's all we'll need from you, but we'll be in touch again if we have other questions. Thanks for your help," she said, getting up.

She and Leblanc headed back to the car, and drove to Circle Drive, which was a couple of miles away, a long, semi-circular road that curved around a park.

They passed through the park and saw that it was still closed to the public until it re-opened in the summer. She glanced toward the gates and saw a sign that said Closed for Winterization. That gave her a sense of this area's isolation. The park was empty and it would be for several months.

They drove past rows of identical cedar sided houses with postage stamp sized front lawns.

Katie slowed down as they reached Circle Drive, and then backed up the driveway to park in front of the front door of number forty.

She and Leblanc both got out, and Katie headed up the path to the door. There was a circular, red stained-glass window installed above the door, which was made of dark wood.

She knocked on the door.

Katie waited. She had a feeling that he wasn't in. The house felt empty. There was mail in the mailbox. She swallowed as she began to wonder whether he'd abducted Sherrie and then fled town. That was a possibility they might need to consider down the line.

For now, to make sure, she knocked again.

They waited. No answer.

"I'm going to circle around to the back. See if he's home," she told Leblanc, who nodded.

She walked around the side of the house, but found only a large fenced in area with a shed. The back door was firmly closed and so were the kitchen curtains.

Katie returned to the front, shivering from her brief walk into the chilly backyard.

"He's definitely not home," she said. "I think we should ask the neighbors if he's been home, and if they have seen him at all."

"I guess we'll have to do that," Leblanc agreed.

Katie turned away, wondering which of the homes to the left and right would be the better bet to start with.

But, at that moment, she heard the purr of a car approaching. She glanced around.

A tan Toyota Corolla was driving slowly down the road.

The car stopped outside the house and Katie felt her heart speed up. Clearly, this was Weaver, who'd been out somewhere and had returned at a very opportune time. She glanced at the plate. The last two letters were definitely the same as the one on the printout. This was their guy. It was time to see if he could answer their questions.

Leblanc took out his badge, heading over to the car. But Katie saw that at the last minute, this driver was aborting his turn into the home. Instead, he swerved back onto the road and accelerated away.

Leblanc stared after him in shock, but Katie was already sprinting for their unmarked.

"He's on the run! He saw we were police and he's trying to escape us! We need to get after him!" she shouted.

Leblanc dove into the passenger seat, and Katie started up the car, thrusting it into gear before speeding off in the direction that Weaver had fled.

She hoped she could catch up with him. There had been no reason for him to drive off so suddenly after clearly seeing a man identifying himself as police.

No reason except guilt.

Gripping the wheel, Katie knew the chase was on.

CHAPTER NINE

She'd gotten away from him.

The driver stared out of the diner's murky glass, taking bites of food he barely tasted. Basic road cuisine. A balancing act between nourishment and poison, most times. Spot the vitamin.

He pushed his milkshake away. It tasted oily and artificial. The burger wasn't much better. The hunger that raged within him, the reason he'd stopped at this well frequented place, wasn't about food.

He'd known that even before detouring here.

He felt the dull ache in his arms as he lifted his coffee cup. That ache had been from lifting her, earlier. If only he'd bothered to check, he would have noticed her hiding place was not adequately secured. He'd made an error, with only himself to blame. He'd let her escape and now regret flamed inside him.

Regret, and loneliness, too. Because now he would have nobody and it would be just as it had been before.

He felt the bite of the cheap metal of the chair as he shifted position. He felt the rasp of his short beard on the collar of his shirt. The driver glanced around, taking in the crowd. This was a busy place. A lot of other drivers – tourists, commuters, truckers, snowplow drivers. All sitting in the booths with their cheerful check tablecloths, and at the long, battered Formica counter.

He tried to gather his resolve for another effort, because he would have to go out looking for her again. He was caught in an endless cycle that he didn't fully understand.

Perhaps this time, she wouldn't have to die. All he needed was the companionship he craved. Why was it so difficult to find? Why did he feel this strange confusion when he thought about it? Why did he feel the need to kill, every time?

His mind veered back to the past, but he couldn't go there. It was blocked to him. His memory wouldn't let him in. It felt as if a gate was closed, firmly. One he couldn't open, and when he began to try, the edges of his sanity felt as if they were fraying. It was a weird feeling, as if his mind was trying to tear itself apart.

Instead, he thought about his present circumstances, and finding her again.

He crammed the last of the burger in his mouth, grimacing at the taste.

"You want more coffee?" The waitress hovered, not even bothering with a smile. She looked tired of working in this cold place, frequented by people she didn't care about, who wolfed down empty calories before heading on their way, invisible and never remembered.

Who would remember him?

Maybe that wasn't the question, the driver thought, but rather who he would remember. Because that would be the only thing that mattered.

"I'm okay thanks," he replied.

Her eyes passed over him, she didn't see him. She would never understand him. Most likely, she would not even recall him if she was asked, and the driver knew that could be a good thing as well as bad.

He slid a twenty under the plate. Way more than the meal was worth, but he didn't want to wait for change. Not when he'd spotted something outside that was grabbing his attention.

He took in the scene, bracing himself because his gut reaction was shock. She'd turned up! She was actually here.

The driver took a deep breath, and then he started to smile.

This was a gift. This was a good omen.

He'd been wondering how he would find her again, but now, here she was. Outside, ready for him to approach her.

He guessed that she must be in need. He'd thought he would have to go out looking for her and instead, she'd come straight to where he was waiting. What did she need? He would tell her he could offer it.

The driver walked out.

He strolled over, not wanting to appear too interested or concerned. He knew instinctively that he must keep under the radar, although he could not remember exactly why. He should not be noticed. Drawing attention to himself in any way would be unwise.

He simply paced outside and took a look at what was happening, out there in the forecourt of this truck stop, that was in an isolated area and yet surprisingly full of activity, with snowy wind gusting over the tarmac.

He watched the woman going from vehicle to vehicle. She was knocking on windows, asking the drivers a question that he couldn't hear because the freezing wind grabbed her words away.

But she looked intent. She looked worried. It was clear she needed something and he was sure it was something he could provide.

She wasn't his type. Did he have a type? Memory stirred, and again he felt that strange splitting sensation in his mind that told him he could not stray too far back, or something might break.

But at any rate, he didn't think she was his type. She was tall for a woman, and she had a serious face. She had mousy blonde hair that was plastered under a woolen hat, but despite the hat, she looked cold.

She was smiling as she went from car to truck to van, But he thought the smile looked forced.

He knew her need, though. That was a certainty. And he had to make sure that he got to her before one of these other drivers did. Or else she would be gone, and he would have to look again.

Despite her height, she was slim, and something about her looked vulnerable. She wasn't from around here, he thought. She had the look of a drifter, someone who'd traveled a thousand other roads in a thousand other towns. The driver liked that. He understood it.

She glanced up, seeing him approaching, hearing him crunching through the snow.

"You look as if you need some help," he said conversationally.

Now, she looked suspicious. He made sure to remain casual, like he didn't really care about her answer.

"Yes, I guess I do. I need a ride."

"You in trouble at all?" he asked. "Need to use a phone?"

"No. No, it's okay. I have a phone. I just need a ride."

"Where are you headed?" he asked.

She told him and he made sure to nod knowingly, even though he barely even heard where she wanted to go, because where she would be going was where he took her.

"I'm not sure I can help you all the way. But I can take you most of the way there for sure," he said. It was a standard reply. Saying he could take her all the way might sound too good to be true, and she might be put off.

"I can't pay you," she said. "I'm broke."

He shrugged. He guessed that having approached her that way, she thought he wanted something.

"I have a daughter a bit younger than you," he explained. "I wouldn't like to think of her out in the cold, trying to get a ride this way. It could be risky. I'm happy to help you out."

The daughter line worked. It had worked for him before. It wasn't true. Or maybe it was, he didn't know. It was in the blankness that he couldn't remember.

But he saw her relax. Those words gave her confidence.

She was going to say yes and then he would have the part that was missing in his life. He felt a new sense of purpose, and a new sense of urgency, the hunger like a raw ache in his body.

She glanced at him again, making eye contact, and he saw her decision being made. She had blue eyes, but they looked shifty. He sensed this woman had secrets. Was she running from something? Out here, with no money and no ride, perhaps she was.

But she wouldn't be able to run from him. He was sure that if she agreed, they would learn to get along. He hoped she would enjoy the ride with him.

This time, he wouldn't become careless. He wouldn't make the mistakes he'd made the last time. He'd learned from those mistakes. Errors had consequences, and he was always open to learning.

"I need to get going now," he said, again being sure to speak casually.

"Okay. Thanks. I'll take the ride," she said.

He felt a flare of triumph, that felt the same as if he'd just completed a successful hunt and brought down his prey.

He had his travel companion, and he was looking forward to the trip.

CHAPTER TEN

Katie accelerated down the road after Weaver, the car fishtailing with the speed. The chase was on. She needed to keep the tan Toyota in her sights, and she had to catch him before he got completely out of view.

"He's guilty. Must be!" Leblanc shouted, bracing himself in the passenger seat.

Clenching her jaw, Katie flattened her foot as they sped around a turn.

The tan Toyota swerved, too, and she could see Weaver was trying to lose them, but running into difficulties on the icy road.

Her eyes narrowed as she took in Weaver's erratic moves. She noted how Leblanc's hands shot out to grip the dashboard as the car slid around another curve and then straightened out. He was a nervous passenger, but in prior chases, they'd both realized that in snowy, icy conditions, Katie was more experienced and had the edge in terms of speed.

She was glad to be in the driver's seat as they raced along at well over the speed limit, but wished she was driving a car that was better equipped for such a fast chase in these conditions, because she was not happy with the grip these tires offered.

The Toyota shot down the road and Katie followed, her gaze fixed on the vehicle up ahead. They were closing the gap. Getting closer.

But then, just as she neared him, the car braked sharply and swerved to the side. Its tires squealed and it rocked unsteadily for a moment. Katie held her breath to see if it would roll, but it didn't. Weaver had managed a hairpin turn and was now flying down a narrow side street.

Katie gritted her teeth, slamming on brakes and twisting the wheel as she followed him. The car fishtailed unnervingly, moving to the side, and she heard Leblanc gasp.

She could not let this guy get away. He knew the area; he was familiar with it. He knew the bolt holes and hiding places, she was sure.

The more distance he gained, the more difficult it would be to find him.

She wasn't about to let him get away.

"We can't let him lose us. If he's the killer, we need to stay on his tail until we know where he's headed. We have to keep track of him."

Out of the corner of her eye, she saw Leblanc grab the radio and call in a request for backup.

"He looks to be headed for the main road," Katie said. She didn't like that he was going that way.

Any road was a danger now. The narrow minor roads carried a huge risk of danger to residents and pedestrians, but the bigger roads, with higher speed, would exponentially increase the risk of a crash. And these roads were icy.

"Keep with him," Leblanc encouraged her, gripping the dashboard once more as she swerved into the fast lane.

Katie had to admit, his instinctive reactions were the tiniest bit hurtful to her as a driver. But then again, she was not loving the thin layer of ice covering the roads. And she was aware of the fact that Weaver was clearly an experienced and skilled driver who was very comfortable in his car, and in this icy environment. Also, as a cab driver, he knew all the roads like the back of his hand. That clever swerve down the side road had almost left her far behind.

Now she realized with a clench of her stomach why he'd joined the main road. He'd done it so that he could weave through the heavier traffic, which he was doing expertly, maneuvering between the slower moving cars and trucks, so that Katie had to bite her lip with tension as she struggled to keep pace with him. Most probably, he was going to take the opportunity to duck down another side road any moment.

She heard Leblanc catch his breath again as a truck swerved into their path, almost colliding with them. Katie wrenched the wheel sideways, feeling her palms slick with tension and her heart firmly in her mouth.

They missed the truck by a hair's breadth. Tires squealed, and horns blared.

The tan Toyota was still speeding recklessly down the road. Weaver was going to kill someone if they didn't catch him soon. She was sure of it.

She had to get him before he got himself.

"It's okay," Katie said, more to herself than Leblanc, as she swerved around another knot of cars. "I got this."

But she didn't know if she had. She was only getting glimpses of the vehicle as it zigzagged in and out between the slower moving traffic, ducking and dodging, as it made its way down the road.

But finally, luck was on her side. The traffic thinned out. She'd managed to keep up. And now, the more powerful police car could start to gain ground on this straight section of road.

He was going to lose this race. Whatever slippery side route he'd planned to take wasn't going to come along quickly enough for him.

Now the police car was flying along. They probably couldn't stop in a hurry and if they hit a patch of ice, it was game over. But she had to get level with him. Gritting her teeth with the tension of doing this precise yet bold move, Katie pulled alongside the Toyota, and then ahead, into his path. She had him trapped now, between the barrier and her car. She saw him swerve desperately and held her ground, her feet ready on the pedals to outmaneuver him.

Then, with a surge of relief, Katie saw another police car, sirens blaring, approaching from behind. Their backup had arrived.

Now, there was nowhere he could run. She slowed gradually, forcing his speed down, until he stopped, pinned between the barrier, her car, and the police car that was flanking him.

The minute their unmarked stopped, Leblanc jumped out, his gun at the ready.

"Out of your vehicle," he yelled.

Katie followed him, still trembling from tension after that knife-edge chase. She barely noticed the blast of cold that hit her as she scrambled out. Their suspect had tried to run, but they had him. Now it was time to find out why he'd fled as soon as he'd seen the police arrive at his home.

*

The interview room at the back of the RCMP office was small and powerfully heated. It felt like walking into a wall of warmth, and Katie was grateful for it as she and Leblanc sat down opposite Weaver.

Face to face with him, she took in his looks and more importantly, his demeanor.

He appeared to be in his late twenties, a stocky man with dark hair and blue eyes. There was an air of desperation about him. His mouth was twitching and his stubby fingers were twining together tightly.

"I haven't done anything wrong," Weaver said, his voice shaking with fear and desperation.

"You fled from law enforcement, Mr. Weaver. That's already a felony," Katie pointed out. "However, we'll get to that offense in due course. Right now, what we're more interested in is why you ran in the first place."

"I - uh - I thought you were going to arrest me," Weaver stammered.

Now they were getting to the bare bones of the argument, Katie hoped.

"And why did you think that?"

"Because I've - look, let me explain. I'm not employed full-time, okay?"

"Your point being?" Katie asked sternly.

"But I still need to put food on the table. So I've been offering rides privately from time to time. You know, taking passengers to and from the airport and suchlike."

"What does that involve?" Leblanc asked him. "Is it not legal, not contractual, or what?"

"It's not allowed; there are rules about it. I had to sign a legal document when I joined. But you know, if a customer wanted a ride off the record, then some of them knew they could call me, then cancel the trip, and I'd come and we'd do a cash deal. So yes, I did a few of those pickups, during my shift, and also sometimes outside of my shift."

He stared at her, looking miserable and guilty.

"So you thought they'd found out?" she asked.

"Yes. When I saw you, I thought they'd figured out what I was doing and sent the cops in to arrest me. I - I panicked. I wish I could rethink all my choices now. I'm so sorry. I've realized how wrong this was. I mean, everything. A lot of what I did was wrong. I'll be a better person going forward. I promise."

Katie considered his words, which rang with a sincerity she didn't think was entirely fake.

He had run for another reason but that did not mean he hadn't abducted Sherrie. Given what he'd been doing with the canceled rides, he'd have had the chance to do exactly that.

"Yesterday evening, you took a woman to the airport. You picked her up from number four, Clover Road."

Weaver looked surprised.

"This is about that?"

"You canceled the fare."

"Yes, yes I did. I remember when I picked her up, she was very angry. She stomped out of the house. She wanted to get to the airport. She had a small bag with her and said she was going to fly back to Minneapolis."

"And then what happened?"

"We'd just set off, when I got a notification her card payment was canceled. The card was maxed out."

"And did you offer her a private deal?"

He looked abashed. "Yes, I did. I said we could work out a cash deal, but she had no cash on her. I said in that case, there's no point in going to the airport. It's a longish drive, you can't book a flight with no money, and how will you get back from the airport? It'll be night time and you'll be stuck there. That's what I said to her."

"And what did she say?"

"She didn't really argue back. I don't think she knew what to do. Now she seemed mad all over again that she had no money. I offered to take her back home again, but she refused; she said she wasn't ever going back there, that she hated her boyfriend. So in the end, I dropped her at the closest mall, near the main road. The Pine Ridge Mall. I don't know what she was going to do there, but I thought at least it's warm and safe and there are people around. I mean, I felt sorry for her."

"Can you prove this version of events?"

"I've got the credit card notification. It came through on my phone; it's synced to do that. I can show you."

Katie handed him the phone and he scrolled through, looking worried.

"Here," he said.

She checked the notification, which looked to be legitimate.

"Where did you go after you dropped her off?"

"I knocked off shift. I went past the grocery store, then home. I messaged a few friends. Organized a meet-up for the evening."

With a shaking finger, he switched to another app and showed her the messages.

Reading them, Katie guessed they cleared him. He'd messaged friends and had then headed out to join them in a bar for the evening.

He hadn't been blasting south, in a vehicle with Sherrie somehow locked away.

But someone had. She had no idea what Sherrie could have gotten up to in the mall. It was a large mall. She could have approached someone inside the mall, or else asked people in the parking lot for a ride. Seeing the mall was near a main road that adjoined the highway, she could even have headed straight onto the main road and tried to hitchhike.

There were too many possibilities to easily explore, and with this being a dead end, Katie knew they were going to have to go back to

Sherrie herself, and hopefully get more information and a clearer version from her if she was able to provide it.

If she was still alive.

Walking out of the interview room, Katie decided to call the hospital, hoping for positive news and for Sherrie to be able to add more to this story.

CHAPTER ELEVEN

Before the call to the hospital could connect, Katie saw she had an incoming call from Scott. Quickly cutting the call to the hospital, she picked up.

"Bad news, I'm afraid," Scott said.

"What's happened?" Katie asked, feeling her stomach lurch.

"Sherrie Blair has died. I just received the call now. Unfortunately her exposure was too severe, and the subsequent effects were fatal. She passed away while on life support, fifteen minutes ago."

Katie felt her heart sink. The poor young woman, who had tried so desperately hard to save herself had, in the end, been claimed by the brutal effects of the bitter cold itself. And now, her harrowing version of events would remain untold.

"I'm so sorry to hear that," she said softly.

"Have you made any progress?" Scott asked.

"We just chased down a lead but it didn't work out," Katie said. "We found out that she was dropped at a local mall after her card was declined on the way to the airport. From there, we still don't know. I was hoping to get more information from Sherrie herself."

"Not going to happen now," Scott said in tones of sad resignation.

"We'll work on it from our side," Katie promised him.

She ended the call.

Leblanc had taken Weaver through to the front desk to process his release. A moment later, he rejoined her. They returned to the interview room, where it was warm, and they could discuss the case.

"Sherrie Blair has died," Katie said, hating the words.

Leblanc shook his head solemnly. "That's sad. And it's complicating for the case. I don't see where this leaves us now. We have no real leads. We don't even know for sure what played out with the victim."

"Something did," Katie said, glaring at him, feeling annoyed that he was doubting the young woman's plight.

Leblanc spread his hands in apology.

"Something happened. For sure, something happened. But we don't know what. She was not in a coherent state when she was found. She could have been mixing up fact and fantasy. We literally do not know how much of what she said was accurate."

"Well, she wasn't injured when she left her boyfriend's home. And she wasn't injured when the cab driver dropped her at the mall. And the only way she could have ended up where she was found was if someone took her there. This was a couple of hours away from The Pas. Not a few miles."

"So someone took her. Or she begged a ride. But this really is not giving us enough to go on. That's the biggest mall in The Pas. It's next to a main road. There would have been literally hundreds of people passing by. I don't know how we can take this further."

"We are going to take it further," Katie snapped. "I'm not letting go of this case until we find out what went on and who took her, or else until we're officially pulled off it."

Leblanc nodded grimly.

"I agree with you. I am not letting go either. But I'm worried this could be a dead end. There is nothing to find."

"We have to try," Katie insisted, her teeth gritted.

She knew Leblanc could see her pain. She knew that he was aware it wasn't just this case, but also the memories of her own loss, that were driving her so strongly to pursue it.

But she wasn't going to compromise and she wasn't going to let go. If he wanted to argue, she was ready to hammer home her side. She wanted an argument with him. Her fighting blood was up.

But, with a small sigh, Leblanc backed down.

"Look, I'm presenting an alternate view just for perspective," he explained. "Because sure as anything, we will also be asked to justify the time we've spent on this. We'll be asked if we are sure we did not waste resources on a pointless investigation."

Katie stared at him, frowning.

"What do you mean?" she asked. She had the feeling Leblanc knew more than he was saying. This was giving her a bad sensation deep down.

But her partner shook his head. "Katie, I don't know. But in the office, a couple of days ago, I overheard Scott having a conversation on the phone with someone and he was talking the way I was just now. As if someone was asking him about that and he was under pressure to explain."

"Do you know who he was speaking to?" Now Katie felt worried.

"I don't have an idea, but I didn't like the tone of the conversation. To me, it felt as if he was having to defend his position." Leblanc shrugged. "But it was not my conversation and I should not have been listening in the first place. I didn't listen for long. I walked away. But I'm just saying, if we continue, we'd better justify why."

Katie nodded.

"I get what you're saying."

Something about what Leblanc was hinting at, made her feel deeply uneasy. She knew the task force had been an experiment initially, but it had then become permanent due to its success and effectiveness. They couldn't do anything to jeopardize its success. If someone was questioning the resources they were using, they could not be seen to be wasting resources without a solid reason and a good motivation.

Uneasy as his words made her, he was absolutely right.

They needed to make sure that every decision they made could be backed up by sufficient proof and reason. They had to be able to justify every action they took.

"One thing that Sherrie definitely said was that this criminal who took her had killed before," she remembered.

"Yes," Leblanc said. "That was something that the man who picked her up clearly recalled her saying."

"It's making me wonder if we should collate the records for the wider area, maybe even the whole of Manitoba. Perhaps there are other missing person cases. Higher than usual numbers, perhaps? More murders in a specific area? Or even something like more women than usual going missing? If there are others, we could track those down. What if there's a pattern to be found? It might even go back years."

Leblanc narrowed his eyes, considering her words.

"That's a good idea. Looking for trends could help us a lot. We could ask the team to research all the records, back at the office in Sault Ste Marie. How far back should we go?"

Katie shook her head. In a recent case they had worked on, the killer had been operational for a number of years.

"We should go back at least four or five years. If nothing else, that will help us to get clear stats and we'll see if anything looks suspicious or at what stage there was a spike. And that's basic research. Basic, cheap research. All it will take is time."

"Good idea. And as for us, what do we do now?"

Looking at his intense features, those dark eyes, Katie felt a surprising flare of emotion.

Leblanc was not just a colleague. He was becoming more. It was only now that he'd dropped this weird hint that the unit was under scrutiny that she realized how much she was appreciating working with him. She didn't want to lose him. It was as simple as that.

The thought of having to go back to her old FBI posting scared her, because it would be like taking a step back into her old life. She loved her new life. Which was ironic, since she'd originally been reluctant to come here. Only a desire to try and solve dangerous crimes with her specialist knowledge of the region had persuaded her to leave her previous investigation team.

"All we have are her words," she reiterated.

"That he'd killed before," Leblanc said.

"And 'driver'," Katie emphasized. "She mentioned the word 'driver'."

"But that's obvious," Leblanc said. "There was no other way for her to have gotten to where she was, than in a car."

Suddenly, an idea occurred to Katie.

"Maybe we're not looking at it in an obvious enough way," she suggested. "The word 'driver' - perhaps it wasn't a description. Perhaps it was the man's actual name. Perhaps she knew it, or learned it. She could have met up with this person at the mall."

Leblanc's eyes lit up. She could see he liked that theory.

"Now that is a possibility," he agreed.

"We need to look through the local records ourselves, also, and see if anyone with the name 'Driver' in this area has a criminal record that might link them up with this offense," Katie decided.

CHAPTER TWELVE

Lizanne watched as the lights of the town flickered past. At last she was in a vehicle, and on the move. Finally, she was putting some distance between herself and her family home in Winnipeg. She'd been worried there for a while. She sure needed to get away. That could have become a bad situation.

Her mother's off-the-record words of wisdom had always been, "Do what you want but don't get caught."

It seemed Lizanne hadn't taken those to heart well enough. She'd gotten caught, and by her own mother, too.

It hadn't been Lizanne's fault. She had tried to help her friend, who admittedly was down and out. Gabby was her old school friend. She'd needed cash. She was trying to get off drugs; she'd promised it was for smokes.

Lizanne had felt so sorry for her. She'd wanted to help. But Gabby had taken the money and bought drugs. And then she'd lied, which had forced Lizanne to lie, and to steal more money from her mom, who'd found out this time.

Her mom had then gone and told Lizanne's dad, who had also freaked out. Then everything had become a big mess.

She'd cried and cried. She felt so upset by everything. She'd begged her dad not to get the police involved because he wanted to call them out to arrest Gabby, once he heard about the drugs. The problem was that Gabby had sold to her a few times and Lizanne knew if she got arrested, Gabby would tell them so, and the police would come for her too.

Her father couldn't let it go, and most times he did what he said he would.

So she'd taken off.

She was going to head to a friend who lived in the far north. Samantha was married to someone who worked in one of the mines. They had extra space and could put her up, and that felt like far enough away from all the trouble that was going to land on her head.

Apparently there were some opportunities in the mine, for cleaning work and such, so she could earn while she was there. It would be like a working vacation and, being so remote, her parents wouldn't be able to pitch up and cause trouble.

Every mile that passed by was taking her further away from the explosion that had lacerated her world.

She stole a look at the driver. He was a quiet guy. Not a talker. He'd barely said a word. But now that she was settled, and her mind had calmed down some, Lizanne was a talker.

"Do you drive this way often?" she asked.

"Every so often."

"Do you live up here somewhere?"

"No."

"Where do you live then?"

"Further down south."

"You got a name?" she then asked.

He shrugged. "I'm just a driver."

This conversation was hard work and it felt strangely awkward. He was answering in a weird tone. She didn't want him to be irritated by her. Lizanne decided she wasn't going to push it. She didn't want to annoy Mr. 'Just a Driver'. She hoped that if she was friendly enough, he might take her the whole way to where she needed to be.

She turned to look back out the window, hoping to see some sign of the small towns and villages that she knew he would be passing through on the way north. Lights were about all she could hope to see in the darkness, of course.

There was a rattling coming from behind the seat. She looked around, wondering what the noise was.

To her surprise, wedged behind the seats, she saw a big wire cage. The kind of cage you'd buy if you had a big breed of dog and you needed to transport the animal.

It looked solid and sturdy. Definitely large enough for a Great Dane, she thought. She liked Great Danes.

"You have a dog?" she asked, craning around to see. But there was no dog in the cage.

Just a dark, tattered blanket at the bottom.

The man gave a deep sigh.

"No. No dog."

Lizanne looked at him. She noticed he had a slightly grim, closed off expression. She watched as his fingers tightened on the wheel.

Lizanne tucked her legs beneath her on the seat. She felt awkward. Something had changed between them. It was like the temperature of the air inside had dropped. There was a strange energy in the vehicle.

She was good at sensing energy. She could pick up on it, and what she was sensing now was weird.

"Did you have a dog?" she asked, aware that she was probably doing what her mother warned her about, and pushing people for information they didn't want to give out. Her mother had said she should not do that. It caused people to snap.

"In the past?" he asked.

"Yes."

"You don't want to know about my past. My past is not for you to know," he warned. "I don't want to speak about it. Speak about something else. But not that."

Lizanne felt uneasy. Something didn't add up with this guy. She was trying to put a finger on what it was. She couldn't quite place it. She really wished now that she'd waited to find another ride.

"My past is also problematic," she said. "My family is mad at me. Do you have a family?"

He shook his head.

"No," he replied.

But then, Lizanne remembered what he'd said to her when he'd approached her outside the diner.

"Wait, what? Yes, you do. You told me you have a daughter. Were you not telling the truth? Do you have a daughter?"

"I can't speak about that," he said.

There was a warning note in his voice but Lizanne ignored it, feeling too irate about the fact he'd tried to fool her. Why had he done such a thing? He'd lied to her! For what reason? She felt completely mad at him for that. Never mind she'd done it quite successfully herself in the past. Other people weren't supposed to.

"You've got a wedding ring. Do you have a wife? Or is that a lie, too? Have you brought me along because you thought I was – I was going to sleep with you or something? Because I'm not like that. I don't do that."

Her motor mouth was running ahead, at full steam, the way it always did when she got really mad.

He turned to look at her and now she didn't recognize the expression in his eyes at all. It was like looking directly into the gaze of an angry stranger.

"I told you not to talk about that. Not to mention it. You're not doing what I asked. You're not doing it, and that means we have to take the next step. It's time. I didn't want to do it so soon, but it's time now."

There was a tone of threat in his voice that she didn't miss. This guy was not normal, Lizanne realized. There was something very, very off about his behavior now.

For the first time, Lizanne felt a flicker of actual fear.

"Let me out!" she demanded. "I don't want to ride with you anymore. Pull over or I'll – I'll call the cops on you."

He gave a strange laugh, cold and somehow disassociated from what she'd said.

"You won't call the cops. From this point, there's no cell signal for the next twenty to thirty miles, because of the alignment of this valley. It's a dead zone that they know about, but they don't do anything about it, because there are no towns nearby, and so few people ride this road. Only when we reach the next town will you be able to pick it up again. By then, it will be too late for you."

Lizanne choked out a gasp. Those words sent a shiver of absolute horror through her. She didn't know what he meant but this sounded really creepy. Horrible.

"Let me out," she said. "Let me out, now, or I promise you I'll jump out!"

"Jump, then. Be my guest. I'll watch you go."

Lizanne turned to the door, struggling with the handle. The thought of plunging out onto the icy tar was terrifying, but right then, it wasn't as scary as spending another moment with this guy, who'd turned into a psycho from her worst nightmares.

But the door wouldn't open. She couldn't open it. It should open, but it didn't. He must have done something to it, so that it was stuck closed from the inside.

And then, sensing movement behind her, she twisted back again, seeing to her horror that he was holding something. That was why he'd let her struggle with the door. So that he could take out this weapon that he was now thrusting at her.

It was something she'd literally only seen in movies. A strange, black, gun-like thing with two metal points.

Taser, her mind screamed at her, it's a taser, he's going to shock you with it, this is why he stopped, he was never going to let you out at all.

She threw herself against the door, screaming.

And then, he lunged at her with the black object, and there was a snapping burn in her neck, a sizzling shock, and she slumped back against the still-closed door.

CHAPTER THIRTEEN

Katie felt determined to follow up on the possibility that Driver was a name, rather than a description. It might be a long shot, but while they waited for any further information to come to light on the historic crime stats they had requested, at least it was something that could be ruled out.

She and Leblanc had decided to check all the recent crime reports in the wider area from Winnipeg to north of The Pas. They were going to look for any evidence that someone with this name either had a recent record, or might be actively engaging in crime within the area.

Settling down to her work, Katie felt a fierce determination to pinpoint this killer. Because now, a killer he was. He might not have killed Sherrie directly, but she had died after getting away from him, and had been convinced that he would have murdered her if she hadn't managed to get away.

How she wished that Sherrie had survived. If she had, finding her killer would be so much easier. But as it was, they had to sift through sparse evidence now, looking for fragments of clues to lead them to this evil man.

Driver.

Had Sherrie learned his name? Had he told her as they traveled, believing it didn't matter because he would kill her? If he had told her, was the name even true? Or had she seen it somewhere or found it out?

That could also have been why she escaped him and ran so desperately, if she'd found out his name, because she might have thought knowing it would get her killed sooner.

They would have to investigate all the possibilities. The area they were looking into was huge and remote. Had the killer been familiar with the area? Or was he just passing through?

He had been in town, though. In town after dark, because Katie guessed that Sherrie would have ended up at the mall in the evening and could have spent an hour or two there trying to find a ride. She might even have gotten one later into the night. But it did indicate that this man had been in the local area – the mall or the main road – at the time.

Beside her, Leblanc was working in silence, and Katie sensed that he was just as affected by Sherrie's death as she was.

Methodically, she collated the information she needed, and then went hunting through the databases, hoping for a match. But it was Leblanc who was first to discover what they were looking for.

"Here, Katie. I have something here," he said, sounding excited.

"What do you have?"

"It's a man called Gideon Driver. According to this record, he works for a furniture removal company that operates throughout Manitoba. And here's the interesting fact: He has a record of violence towards women."

"A furniture removal company?" Katie felt intrigued. That fit the puzzle piece they were looking for in terms of his mobility through the area. "And what crime record does he have?"

Scooting her chair closer, she looked at the screen.

"Two years ago, assault of his girlfriend while drunk. He broke her arm, punched her repeatedly, and locked her into the bathroom. He served a few months for that. And it says here there were earlier charges filed by his ex-wife, but due to insufficient proof, he never served time for them."

"Now that is interesting."

Katie read through the report, feeling as if they were on the right track. Not only did Gideon Driver have the record of violence that she thought they might find, but he'd also locked his ex-girlfriend away. That pointed to the same behavior pattern that the killer had shown, even though she didn't know where or how he'd locked Sherrie away.

And the level of violence in the attack was significant.

"He sounds worth investigating. Where does he live?"

"Right here in The Pas," Leblanc said, sounding as excited as Katie now felt. This suspect, in all likelihood, had been in the area when Sherrie had been trying to get back home. Perhaps he'd opportunistically grabbed her, or else had been heading that way and taken her along.

"We need to go and speak to him. What's his address?"

"I'll look it up now," Leblanc said.

As he got busy with the research, Katie's phone rang.

Seeing Scott's name on the caller ID, she grabbed it hurriedly. She couldn't repress a surge of fear that the killer had struck again, and he was phoning to tell her the worst.

But it seemed he was calling for a different reason. She knew as soon as she picked up.

She could hear the tone in his voice was hopeful, rather than the heavy tone that she'd learned he used when bringing bad news.

"There's a possible lead here, Katie. I've been following the crime reports live in case anything relevant comes up. And there's just been a report called in. A woman has called the police and said she was attacked at a truck rest stop."

"What, just now?" Katie asked, feeling excited.

"Yes. I've got an open line to all the crimes being called in, in the wider area, so we can monitor anything relevant. I've checked the location, and this truck stop is about fifty miles south of where you are now, so it's right in our area of focus. The woman is on the scene with the owner in attendance, and police are on their way. She said the man tried to drag her to his car, apparently."

"We'll follow up on that," Katie said.

She cut the call and turned to Leblanc.

"There's another possibility. There's just been an attack on a woman at a truck stop fifty miles south. Sounds like an attempted abduction."

Leblanc's eyebrows shot up.

"So the attacker got away? Do they know more?"

"Not yet. Police are on the way. Scott gave us a heads-up. Both these leads are important. We have one car. What shall we do?"

"I think I should take the car, and go to the truck stop. There's pressure of time there and we need to be on that scene as fast as possible so that we can try and track the guy who attacked her."

"Agreed," Katie said.

"In that case, you can go and interview Driver, who's locally based. We can speak to the officers in the department here, and borrow another car to use for that trip," Leblanc suggested.

Katie would have liked to go out to the truck stop herself, but she knew that Leblanc would want to handle the situation he perceived as being more volatile and unknown. He'd done that in their previous serious case.

He wanted to prove himself, to shoulder the danger, to take on more than his mandate, and Katie also knew why. She knew what he'd recently been through and the emotional upheaval he'd had to handle as he processed the remnants of his own grief over the loss of his ex-lover.

He'd almost gone down a dark road. She sensed that now, he'd regained control of his life and wanted to prove his dedication to himself as well as to her.

At the last moment, Leblanc had redeemed himself. Volunteering for the riskier of the two choices was a way of showing he was back on track and willing to shoulder the full responsibility of his job.

She didn't resent him for it. Leblanc's courage was one of the qualities she most admired about him. He'd never back down from a dangerous situation, and it made him a partner that she could trust implicitly when they were on a risky case.

"That sounds good," she said. "That's a sensible way of using the resources we have. I'll ask Scott to send you the coordinates."

"We can connect again as soon as we both know more. Let me get going now."

Leblanc leaped up, grabbed his laptop and the car keys, and headed out the door at a run.

Katie hoped that one of them would get results. They needed them. The worst thing they could face now would be a stalled case. She could feel the urgency burning like a brand within her.

She was determined to bring down this killer, and avenge Sherrie's death.

But she also knew that when they were dealing with killers, in these icy and remote parts of the world, there was no such thing as a guarantee of safety.

Any moment in a case could turn deadly. There was no certainty that her own interview would be safe or routine.

She would need to be prepared for any eventuality, as she headed out to find the violent Gideon Driver.

CHAPTER FOURTEEN

Speeding along the road in the police cruiser that she'd borrowed from The Pas police department, Katie headed out to Gideon Driver's recorded address.

It was already dark, she saw, with a shiver of worry. Their research had been time consuming. Databases had been slow. Now, it was six p.m. and night was approaching.

They'd spent the day chasing down information and leads, but with the death of their victim, Katie felt as if they'd suffered nothing but setbacks. She hoped that either she or Leblanc would pick up solid evidence, or maybe even the killer himself.

Gideon Driver lived on the extreme outskirts of The Pas. The area was a mix of small farms, forest, and mountains, and it was just a short drive to the nearest highway.

As she left the main road and wound her way along the potholed track that led to his home, Katie was struck once again by how bleak and cold it still was here. It felt like the depths of winter had descended. Clouds were starting to build, and she wondered if a snowstorm was slowly brewing.

She pulled up outside Driver's place and took a look at the simple house, with a plain white fence, a small front yard, and a basic garden. The house was old, and looked to be suffering from signs of neglect. She saw grimy window glass, a dead plant in a planter near the door, and a few places where the fence was starting to splinter.

The path was swept, though, smooth and clean and free from snow.

Katie climbed out of the cruiser and walked to the front door.

She knocked, making sure that she remained ready for any eventuality. Experience had taught her that in these out of the way places, people were often deeply suspicious of the police, or even outright aggressive toward them.

But there was no answer.

She couldn't see a light inside. She walked a few steps around the house and saw that the lean-to which clearly housed a vehicle, was empty, with tire tracks cutting through the snow. So he wasn't here, but looked to have recently left.

Were any neighbors around?

Katie walked to the fence, taking a look at the cottages to the left and right of this property.

The one to the left was dark. She could see no lights and guessed that these residents were also not home.

The one to the right looked to be occupied. There was a light inside, and she walked closer, feeling hopeful.

She knocked on the door and, after a moment, heard footsteps approaching.

"Hello," she called as the door was opened, and a woman peered out at her. She was in her fifties, and looked nervous and surprised to see Katie there. From inside the house, a fire crackled, and she smelled the rich aroma of cooking meat, but the welcome on the doorstep was not so warm.

"What do you want?" the woman asked, sounding defensive and wary.

"I'm a police investigator getting information on a recent crime. I'm looking for your neighbor, Gideon Driver," Katie said. "Do you know where he might be now?"

"Is he a criminal?" the woman asked, casting a suspicious glance in the direction of his house.

"There's no proof of that, ma'am. We simply need information from him."

"He's not here," the woman said. "I saw him come home earlier and go out again."

"Do you know when he'll be back?" Katie asked.

"No, I don't," the woman said.

"Do you know him well?" Katie asked.

"I know him as well as I want to know him," the woman said, looking at Katie grimly. She got the distinct feeling that this woman didn't like or trust her neighbor. The problem was that she clearly also didn't like or trust Katie.

"Do you know where he might be, at this hour? Perhaps he heads somewhere local in the evening?" Katie tried, thinking that if she could ask better questions, it might make it easier for the woman to tell her.

She was silent for a while. Katie thought she wasn't going to say, but then she seemed to change her mind.

"There's a bar at the corner of the road, about a mile down. Sometimes when I pass by, I see his car stopped there in the evenings. It's an old Land Rover. But if he's not there, I don't know where he is. And I'd rather you didn't mention I told you that."

"Thank you," Katie said. "If I find him, I won't mention it to him."

She decided not to quiz the woman further. Katie got the impression that she didn't want to be on Driver's wrong side. After all, she had to live next door to him. Katie didn't.

Climbing back into the police cruiser, Katie traveled back down the windswept road to the building she'd noticed as she'd turned onto this lane. There were several cars outside. Including a Land Rover that clearly fitted the description of 'old', parked on the snow-covered sidewalk.

She guessed that thanks to its location close by, this rather dilapidated looking drinking hole was a regular haunt for Driver.

Katie got out of the car. She could hear music thumping from inside the bar. Smoke issued from the chimney. Before she even walked inside, she already knew how it would smell, thick with wood smoke and cigarette smoke and the aroma of beer and whisky.

She recalled the ID photo of Driver, which was fairly recent. He was a short, strong looking man, with dark hair and eyes, and heavy, dark brows.

Glancing through the glass as she passed the window, she saw all the patrons were men, and seemed to be clustered around the bar itself. Two younger men were at a table in a corner, playing pool. She had the feeling she would be walking into an enclave of locals, and expected straight away that this would not be easy.

The fact she was police would not make any difference, other than to increase their levels of disrespect.

But at least Katie knew she was forewarned, and had the chance to prepare herself.

Katie stepped into the bar, and took in the surroundings quickly. There were about eight men inside, all drinking, laughing, and passing the time. All were dressed in winter jackets, jeans, and boots. Most of them had the look of men who worked outdoors in this rugged environment, with wind-chapped faces.

She saw no welcome in any of their eyes.

A gust of cold wind blew in with her, but she already knew the response she was going to receive was even more frigid.

There was Driver, sitting near the end of the bar. She recognized those heavy features easily from the ID photo she'd examined earlier.

Katie walked toward him, aware of the cold stares and the fact that the bar had now fallen silent. Everyone had stopped talking to watch her, including the young, tough-looking barman who was staring at her suspiciously.

She heard a muttered comment from behind her and a snigger of laughter.

"Gideon Driver?" Katie asked politely, walking up to him.

He was seated on a bar stool with a bottle of beer in front of him.

He looked at her through narrowed eyes.

"That's me," he said slowly.

"I'm FBI Agent Winter." She showed her badge, more for formality's sake than because she felt it would make any difference. "I need to ask you some questions regarding a recent crime. I'm looking for information. Would you speak to me for a moment?"

She didn't want to come across as hard core. She wanted to give him the choice. But she knew already what his choice was going to be. She could see it in his eyes, in the scorn with which he regarded her.

It told her all she needed to know about what Driver thought of women, and police. She was both.

He wasn't going to cooperate with her at all.

"Well, now, little lady," he said, and Katie had to make an effort to keep her expression calm when hearing his insulting tone.

There were more sniggers from his friends.

"It seems we have a situation here. Because I've done nothing wrong. I've got no reason to be interviewed by the police. And I've got nothing to say to you. So if you want me to answer any questions, I suggest you make me."

He grinned at her, a wide grin, showing yellowed teeth. Then he glanced at his friends, who nodded their approval.

"Make him," one of them laughed. "Or maybe we make you get out. Wasting our time!"

The challenge was down.

She was one woman against a group of men who were not going to lift a finger to help her.

Driver thought he was invulnerable and he disrespected her. And, if she wanted to get anywhere, Katie knew she was going to have to make him.

CHAPTER FIFTEEN

Leblanc had been driving for half an hour, trying to channel Katie's skill in winter conditions as he sped along the roads, feeling both hopeful and apprehensive about what he might find at the truck stop. It could well be that the killer was out there, opportunistically seizing the moment. But not every attempt would go his way. It could be that he hadn't managed to abduct this woman successfully. Perhaps other people had seen and intervened, or she'd been able to fight him off for long enough that he fled.

He hoped that he could catch up with this criminal and that he'd conduct himself in an exemplary way. Right now, as a unit, they could not afford to make mistakes.

By turning down the Paris job offer, Leblanc had just given up what was, undoubtedly, an upward career move. He'd done so for the right reasons. It had been an ethical choice.

But what terrible irony it would be, if the unit he'd chosen to stay with got its budget slashed, or was downsized, or 'absorbed' to become meaningless, or any other of the fates that Leblanc knew could befall any unit if the powers that be started with their political shenanigans.

Then how would he feel?

He'd turned down the senior opportunity - partly because Katie had been absolutely right in that his reason for taking it had been wrong, but also because he was loyal to their unit. He felt close to every single one of the professionals he worked with. They were top caliber people - skilled, intelligent, brave. He was proud to be a part of a task force solving crimes that up until now had a low solve rate thanks to the unique challenges of the northern area.

And then there was Katie herself. He knew he was becoming too involved with her, too close.

The thought of becoming closer made warmth flare in his heart. But it also created a sense of fear, because he knew what could happen when things went wrong with a case partner.

He couldn't face losing another partner he was close to, when a case went bad.

Leblanc's focus was wrenched back to the task at hand by the notification that he was nearing his destination.

Now it would be time to see if the attacker could be tracked down, and if he was the criminal they were hunting.

He felt hopeful that if it was, this case could be put to bed. Closed. A criminal caught. Nothing could bring Sherrie back, but at least no others would be at risk from this rogue killer that, as yet, they knew little about.

Immediately, Leblanc saw police were on the scene. The RCMP vehicle was parked near the convenience store and rest rooms. There were a few other cars and trucks at the stop, and a couple of men were standing around in the dark of evening, in the pools of light from the overhead lamps. Swathed in coats, they were looking curiously at the scene.

He parked alongside the RCMP car, and climbed out. The cold was immediately biting.

"Detective Leblanc," he said, walking over to the scene.

The woman was standing with two RCMP officers who Leblanc guessed had recently arrived as one was still busy taking notes. The woman appeared to be in her thirties. She was plump-faced and blonde-haired. She looked defiant and also a bit defensive, he thought, wondering exactly what had happened here.

"Good evening," the RCMP officer said. "I've just taken a statement from the victim, Shiree Jacobsen."

The blonde-haired woman was keen to repeat it again. She turned to Leblanc, speaking in a loud, angry voice.

"I was on my way to the restroom when this guy tried to attack me. He tried to grab me! I twisted away and started screaming, and he then drove off in a hurry."

"Can you describe him?" Leblanc asked Shiree.

"He was young. Maybe thirty. Tall. Strong looking. He was wearing a black jacket, jeans, and had a hoodie over his head."

"What kind of vehicle did he drive?" Leblanc asked. "Did you note the vehicle, ma'am?"

"A silver SUV. I'm not sure of the type, but I am sure of the color. He grabbed my arm and tried to drag me to the car. I had to fight him off." She glared at him mutinously. "Then he jumped into the car and drove away."

Immediately, Leblanc saw that this type of vehicle would be big enough to keep a victim locked away in the back. This was sounding as if it was adding up.

"He headed north, according to Ms. Jacobsen's witness report," the RCMP officer explained. "We've alerted police in the nearby towns.

We've already asked the truck stop attendant to look up the plate. It should be visible from the camera footage."

At that moment, a man in a bulky jacket, who Leblanc guessed was the attendant, hurried out of the small store.

"I've picked up the plate footage if you want to view it."

Quickly, they hurried into the side office, where Leblanc's face started tingling in the overly warm interior after the windy cold outside.

"It's a Manitoba plate," he said, peering at the screen where the silver SUV was clearly visible as it departed. Unfortunately, the camera angle did not show the attack itself. It seems these cameras were focused only on the vehicles in the small parking lot and at the gas pumps.

"If it's a Manitoba plate, then our man is a local, seems like," the officer agreed. "I'll get the word out to the control room, and if he's the registered owner, we will hopefully be able to pick up his address details."

With the plate information in hand, and nothing further to be gleaned from the site itself, Leblanc decided to start driving north. That was where the attacker had headed and the sooner he got on the road, the closer he might end up being when the address was called in.

"Let's stay in touch," he said. "Radio me as soon as you know more."

He climbed in the car and began the drive north, hoping that he would be ready to catch this man as soon as they had a positive ID and address for him.

*

After Leblanc had driven for ten minutes, his cruiser's radio suddenly crackled to life and Leblanc felt his hands tense on the wheel.

"The registered owner of the vehicle has been located. His name is Charles Burn, and he lives in a town called Lakeside at eight Blossom Avenue."

Excited, Leblanc checked his map, feeling glad that he'd made the decision to start driving. Lakeside was just five miles away. In fact, he'd just passed it and needed to go back.

"I can be there in a few minutes."

Checking his mirrors, Leblanc swerved the car in a tight turn and accelerated back the way he'd come.

As he drove, he wondered what would play out when he reached the man who hopefully was the vehicle's registered owner. He needed to be ready for anything.

The man might be armed. He might decide to take a stand. Or he might decide to flee in which case Leblanc would have to be ready for the chase.

All those scenarios had played out in Leblanc's mind, ever since he'd been given the call. He needed to be ready for anything. He drove carefully, watching the road, the scenery, and his rear view mirror.

Whatever happened, he was committed to it.

As he approached Lakeside, he saw that it was a small town, no more than a village. He guessed it was next to a lake, though in the dark the scenery was invisible. Lights illuminated a cluster of houses and a few businesses, including a hotel and a restaurant.

He got on the radio.

"I'm entering the town. I'm looking out for Blossom Avenue, and also for the vehicle, in case he hasn't yet gone home."

The description of the car, and the number plate, was on the top of his mind. In this small town he didn't think it would be difficult to locate him, and there was only one main exit point, which was back to the highway.

There it was!

"I've seen him!" he said. In the glow of the street lamp, he'd caught a glimpse of a silver SUV ahead. He managed to pick up the last three digits of the plate, which was good enough to convince him.

"The suspect is in sight," he said, picking up speed as he drove past the old-fashioned gas pumps.

The SUV had pulled out of a small strip mall. Its headlamps were on, and it was clear that he was heading out of town along a road leading to the remote farmland beyond. Checking the map, Leblanc saw this suspect was now heading to his recorded address.

Leblanc flattened his foot as he tried to follow the SUV, which was now speeding through the town's streets.

The vehicle was going suspiciously fast, and he was aware that he didn't have backup, which made him worried about losing this lead. Had Charles picked up that he was being followed?

The SUV continued north, out of town. Leblanc followed, his hands tight on the wheel. Then it veered off from the main road onto a smaller side road. Leblanc swerved to follow. At least this road didn't seem to lead anywhere except to the farms beyond.

The scenery was remote, pitch black, and the roads were quiet. The SUV was powering through the turns. The driver was clearly familiar with his home turf.

Ahead, the SUV's brakes flashed red. He was stopping. He was turning into one of the small homes.

Leblanc gasped as he saw the man race from the car to the front door and burst into the house. The door slammed behind him.

Pulling up outside the gate, Leblanc followed suit, adrenaline surging. Sprinting for the house, groping for his gun, he reached the front door. He hammered on it hard.

"Police!" he yelled. "Open up!"

The door was flung open almost immediately. Then, to his shock, he came face to face with a red haired woman, wearing a tracksuit and slippers and an equally flabbergasted expression.

She let out a cry of surprise.

"What's happening! Charles, someone's followed you! We're being robbed!" she shouted.

"No, no, ma'am," Leblanc hastened to correct her. "I'm police. The driver who has just entered your home is suspected of being involved in an incident earlier at a truck stop."

"Charles?" the woman called again, now sounding utterly confused.

Leblanc heard a toilet flush from further inside the house. The reason for the man's hasty sprint inside was becoming apparent.

Footsteps sounded, and the man walked back to the front door, looking confused.

"What's happening? I just got home."

He was a dark haired man in his early thirties, broad shouldered and strongly built. He matched the victim's description of her attacker, but Leblanc was surprised by the honest puzzlement in his pleasant face.

"We have a report that you assaulted a woman at a truck stop earlier this evening," Leblanc said.

The man frowned. "Me?" he said incredulously. "I think you've got the wrong guy."

"You stopped at the truck stop south of here. The victim then complained that you'd tried to attack her?"

Light dawned on his face.

"Oh, that? I didn't attack her. But I noticed she was parked in the wrong place and I asked her to move because her car was blocking the exit and trucks would have a problem leaving. She got very argumentative and abusive, and refused. I said if she didn't move the car, I would take the keys and move it myself."

"That's what happened?" Leblanc asked.

"Yes. She started yelling and screaming at me, but she did then move the car. I decided to leave. I needed the bathroom, but didn't want to get into a fight with her and she looked like she wanted to fight. I can't believe she called the cops. That's just weird."

"Can you prove your version?" Leblanc asked.

"Sure. I have a dashcam. I think some of it would have been captured on that. I can get it for you now, if you like?"

Leblanc decided that the presence of the dashcam, together with the honest offer of providing the footage, confirmed his version that the blonde had been trying to get the last word in an argument through a clearly false accusation. Even so, he was determined to get the full picture.

"It won't be necessary, but I'd like to know about your movements last night. Where were you?"

He looked surprised. "Last night? I was on shift. I'm a paramedic. I was on duty from six p.m. to six a.m. with my team. We had a few callouts. Today is my day off, and tomorrow, I'm back on duty at six p.m. again."

"Thank you," Leblanc said.

He left feeling disappointed. This promising lead had fizzled into a complete dead end.

His thoughts turned to Katie. He imagined that he was the one heading into danger. But, in fact, his suspect had been an ordinary family guy.

What was happening with her situation, he wondered anxiously.

CHAPTER SIXTEEN

"Make me," Driver said to Katie a second time, grinning at her in a disrespectful way. Around her in the bar, she picked up both jeers and scornful stares.

"All right," she said. "I will make you."

She took a moment to check Driver out. He was bigger and stronger than her, but she guessed she would be faster. She was sober and she didn't think he was. Being drunk would slow him.

And she was trained.

She waited for her chance, taking the time to find the best way to take him on.

"You're gonna make me?" he sneered. "How?"

He was grinning at her, enjoying the prospect of a fight. But she'd been in situations like this before, and she knew how the scene might play out. She needed to wait, and then move fast. She had to show strength and speed. She had to act in a way that intimidated the other patrons, because if she didn't, then they would weigh in with the fight. In a place like this, sentiment could turn on a dime. She didn't want to find herself the victim.

"Come on, Driver," someone shouted, clearly enjoying the exchange.

"Back off," he threatened. "You're not wanted here, and I'm not speaking to you."

She looked around the room. There was no sign of help. That was another thing to consider. She had to make this work on her own.

He was leaning against the bar. A bottle of beer was in his big hand. He was slowly swigging it, still grinning at her. Then he put the bottle down.

"Get out," he said. "I've said I'm not coming with you. That's final."

He stepped toward her. That was good. She was happy to let him try to physically remove her, because it would provide even more reason for his subsequent arrest.

She let him come close and lunged in to meet him. As he raised his hands to grab her, she punched him hard in the gut.

Speed. Shock value.

He let out an oomph of surprise, and bent over to clutch his stomach. But he didn't stay there for long. Clearly, he was strong and aggressive and no stranger to a fight. She didn't have the chance to get hold of his arm before he attacked again.

"You bitch," he grunted, lunging to grab her.

She ducked, avoiding his hands. She kicked his knee and he yelled, surprised and angry.

"That's it! That's it!" he yelled, coming at her in a fury with fists swinging. He almost got in a lucky blow, but at the last moment she dodged again, and the fight was on.

Now she was ready. She was sure he'd be as violent as he was arrogant, but he was not fast. He was drunk and he was slow.

She was fast, moving and thinking on her feet. He was bigger, but uncoordinated. He charged again, blundering toward her, his arms swinging wildly. If he connected with her, she'd go down. No doubt about it. But she avoided his attack, and timing her move, she jumped at him. This time, she got her right arm around him, pinning his flailing left arm to his side, ducking away from the blows he was trying to rain on her with his right.

From around her, she heard shouts and cries. She kicked his knees again, wanting him off balance. Staggering back, he crashed into a bar stool that clattered to the ground. The other patrons were moving away, clearing the area. They weren't rushing in to help him.

But the fight wasn't over. Even as she tried to grab him again, he caught her, wrenching out of her grasp as he tried to throw her down.

But she was fast and lucky, because there was nothing behind her as she reeled back, and she was able to quickly regain her footing and balance. She leaped toward him, using her speed to help with the force of the attack. Wrapping her arm around him, grabbing his throat, she shoved him toward the bar. His own momentum drove him toward the wooden counter, and he slammed into it.

Maddened, he swung at her with force. She ducked and punched him hard in the gut again. He went down, clutching his stomach, his face screwed up with pain.

Katie didn't hesitate. The fight was out of him. She'd managed to subdue him with the minimum of time and injury. She hadn't wanted to hurt him badly. After all, she needed to speak to him.

But she was going to hurt him bad enough to make sure he didn't try any further moves.

While he was still gasping, she took his arm and wrenched it up behind his back so that he cried out again.

Then, while she still had him trapped in that hold, she got the cuffs from her belt, clipping one over the wrist she had in her grasp, and then yanking his other hand behind him. He thrashed, shouting and kicking out, but she twisted his arm up again and he subsided with a groan.

She pushed him against the bar again, and cuffed his other wrist. He was moaning, bent double with pain.

"You hurt me," he said.

She ignored him, breathing hard, turning to see the bartender watching her nervously, as if hoping she wouldn't get mad at him, or anyone else.

"I'm taking him in," she said.

There was a stunned silence at the bar.

A space had cleared around them, a gap a couple of yards wide. Katie noted nobody was trying to close that gap. Everyone was suddenly being very respectful. There were no more sniggers to be heard.

She was out of breath from the intense fight, but she wasn't in a bad way, like Driver was. Driver was still trying to get his wind back from her second punch in the gut. Katie was pleased by how well it had gone. But then, he was clearly surprised by her techniques.

She turned him and pushed him outside, half-holding him up as he stumbled to the car in the dark, cold evening. She got him in the back seat, hooked his cuffs to the clip so he couldn't make a run for it, and headed for the RCMP department.

*

Fifteen minutes later, Katie walked into the interview room where Driver was waiting.

He'd recovered somewhat from his short ordeal at her hands, although he was still stooped over, and had a graze on his cheek.

"What was that about?" he asked in tones that told her he was feeling sorry for himself. Now that the bully had been bested, he was resorting to self-pity.

"Next time, cooperate with the police," Katie told him shortly. She didn't have time for idiots who thought they could take the law into their own hands.

"What do you want from me?" he asked sullenly.

"We had a victim of abduction end up in the hospital at Winnipeg. She was found on the highway a few hours' drive north. She got away from the man who'd taken her. She spoke the word 'Driver'. So we're following up on people with that name in the area, who have a record. Such as yourself," Katie explained.

His eyes flew wide. He looked horrified and afraid. "A woman was abducted?" he yelped. "I don't know nothing about that. I swear it, I wouldn't do something like that."

"She mentioned the name 'Driver'," Katie said.

"It wasn't me, seriously!" he protested. "Please tell me you believe me. I don't want to end up framed for something I never did."

He was practically pleading with Katie. He seemed afraid that he was in real trouble now.

"What were your movements yesterday? I want an account of where you were, and when," Katie pressured him. She needed to know if he would have had any window of opportunity to take Sherrie.

He looked upset. "I worked from eight to five. My day job."

"Doing what?"

"I work for a removals company. I deliver stuff. Furniture, white goods, that sort of thing."

"Were you on the road yesterday?"

"Yesterday, we were doing a job within town. In The Pas. Here's the address details, on my phone. But I didn't do the driving. I went along with one of the other guys to help lift and carry, for an office move from downtown to the suburbs. We began at eight, and were done just before seven p.m. I called my manager to tell him we were knocking off. Here's the call I made."

"And then?"

"Then I went to the bar. I can confirm I was there last night until they closed at eleven. I played a few games of pool. Bought food and drinks. Used my card. I'll show you the slips, I think they are still in my wallet."

With hands now shaking, he fumbled in the wallet and produced a crumpled paper. He unfolded it, and Katie saw the credit card slips from the bar. Katie took them, scanned them briefly. He'd been there, all right.

"Okay," Katie said.

"I'm not the kind of guy who would do something like that," he explained. "I'm sorry I gave you a hard time."

Reluctantly, Katie saw she would have to rule out this witness. He did have a confirmed alibi and his time when Sherrie had been taken was accounted for. He wasn't entirely innocent and was a troublemaker for sure. But he was not the criminal they were seeking.

Katie felt very uneasy about this because it meant they had so far come up blank in their search.

She hoped that by tomorrow morning, they would have the historic crime records that the task force was busy compiling, because it was the only lead she could think of that might allow them to move forward with the case.

It always made her nervous to have to leave a case at night. There was always a chance that things could go wrong. Always, she feared that by the morning, there would be more bad news.

CHAPTER SEVENTEEN

Lizanne opened her eyes. They hurt. Her head was aching. Her neck was on fire.

And worst of all, she was a prisoner. She stared up at the crisscrossed steel bars above her head.

She was in the cage she'd seen behind the seat. He'd shocked her and knocked her out and put her in this cramped prison. Lizanne didn't know how long she'd been unconscious. One moment she was sitting next to him, and the next moment she was in this cage. He had taken her coat away, and put her in this cage.

Lizanne let out a cry of terror.

It was as if he hadn't heard. Craning her neck, she could see him sitting at the wheel.

It was pitch dark and she guessed it was deep into the night.

He had her in total isolation. There was nobody else around. She was alone with him, and trapped in this cage.

She began to tremble uncontrollably.

"Let me out!" she shouted, her voice quivering. "This isn't fair! Let me out!"

He didn't answer. He didn't even look around. He was sitting at the wheel, staring ahead. She couldn't see his face. She saw a dark shadow, nothing more.

"Tell me about your day," he said.

His voice was weirdly intimate.

"My - what?" she said.

"Your day. Tell me about your day," he repeated.

"You mean - ?" she didn't understand what he was asking.

"What were you doing today?" he said, his tone expectant.

Confused, she grasped that he was taking part in some sort of weird dialogue. She'd sensed that strangeness earlier. He was odd. He seemed totally confused. It was like he blanked out when she'd asked him innocent questions. And now she was his prisoner, and he was bizarrely asking her to talk about her day.

"I don't know what you mean! How can I tell you anything?" she asked, hearing the stress thrumming in her own voice. "You've locked me in here. You're like - a psycho. And now I must talk to you?"

"Tell me about the last day you worked." It was as if he hadn't heard her or wasn't listening.

"I haven't worked for ages," she said. "The last job I took, I was fired from. They said I had a bad attitude. And maybe I do. I'm not going to start talking to you anyway."

The road they were on felt uneven and dangerous. It seemed to be totally frozen. She could feel herself rocking from side to side, and she could hear the ice hissing under the wheels and feel the occasional slip and slide as they lost purchase.

"What was the job?" he asked. "You need to tell me something. That's why you're here. You need to tell me. You need to do what I want you to do!"

"I can't tell you," she spat. She was beginning to panic. She had no idea what he was trying to do. Was he trying to get her to trust him? Why was he even doing this?

He was bad, evil. She didn't know where she was or what was going to happen. She was at his mercy.

"Why did they fire you?" he asked.

"They said I don't follow instructions," she said. "I'm not a good worker."

She heard the wind howling outside. There was a loud crack, like ice shattering, and she jumped.

He let out a weird laugh. "Not a good worker," he said. "You should have been a good worker, I guess. What happened when they fired you?"

"I - I don't feel good. I don't want to talk to you. I'm nervous."

That wasn't true. She wasn't nervous. Not really. She was terrified. Her fingers explored the cage. Was there a way out? Could she force her way out of this wire prison?

"Did you talk to anybody?" He sounded interested.

She was close to tears with frustration. "I don't know what you want me to say, or why you're even telling me this. I'm cold and I'm scared. I just want out of here. Let me out!"

"What is your name?" he demanded.

"None of your business," Lizanne snapped. "If you think you are striking up a friendship, then you have another think coming. I have nothing to say to you. Nothing! You're a psycho."

Fear surged through her. She knew there was something terribly wrong with this man. He looked strong and fit; she'd have no chance to get away from him if he decided to hurt her.

He was so aggressive, so weird. She felt that he could do anything. And that he would.

Her body was shaking with terror. And from the cold. She was wearing only her sweater and jeans, because he'd taken her coat.

"Why did you pick me up?" she whimpered.

"I've been wondering the same thing," he said. "I'm sure I don't know the answer now. I'm thinking you're the wrong person. Not the right one for me."

She wasn't sure she understood him.

It was so dark outside. There was nobody around. Nobody to hear her. Nobody to help her.

She was alone with this madman.

Lizanne could feel herself beginning to cry. She tried to hold back the tears, but they welled up and spilled over anyway.

"Please let me out," she begged.

"I'm thinking about that," he said.

"Just let me go! I hate you. You're an ugly man, you're some kind of psycho murderer, and you're scaring me! Why are you doing this? Are you getting your crazy kicks from it?"

"I'm not a murderer," he said. "I wasn't, anyway. I never meant to be."

"I don't know what you are," she sobbed. "I'm going to die. I'm going to die, being in here like this. What are you doing to me?"

She was afraid that he would never let her go. She could feel the cold through the bars of the cage, and there was no other place to go. He was taking her somewhere. He had her trapped in this cage.

His silence stretched on and on. Lizanne stared up at the bars of the prison and tried to get herself under control. She wiped her tears away and drew her knees up to her chin and hugged herself, trying to get warm.

"Why did you take me?" she repeated, her voice breaking.

"I don't know," he said, in a strange voice. He sounded so odd. "I just needed you, but I am not sure now it was the right decision."

"Please just tell me, who are you? What do you want? Where are you going to take me?" She was pleading.

"I don't know how it is," he replied. "I just like talking to you. Tell me about your day. Why won't you do that? It's surely simple enough?"

"You're crazy," she whispered. "You're out of your mind. I'm going to die, if you don't let me out. I'm not going to talk to you. Screw you."

And then, she heard him give a resigned sigh.

He slowed down. She heard brakes wailing.

"I'm sorry," he said. "You're right. It's not working out."

With a flash of fear, and too late, Lizanne realized that complaining had been the wrong thing to do.

Definitely the wrong thing to do.

Her insides turned to water as she heard the words. This was it. He was going to kill her now.

"I'm sorry," he said again. "I don't know where this went wrong. You're not saying what I need you to. You're being ugly to me. I'm sorry."

He stopped. She could feel the engine ticking to a halt. Her heart was in her throat.

He turned to her, his big hands opening the cage.

"I'm sorry," he said, his voice deep and quiet. "I'm going to have to kill you. But you don't need to worry. You won't feel anything at all."

There was the taser. Its dark bulk loomed.

An electric spark, and that was the last thing she knew.

CHAPTER EIGHTEEN

Katie sat in the dining room of the small hotel in The Pas where she'd booked two rooms. There was nothing more to do now. Nothing but rest, refuel, and wait for the results that might take them a step further.

She read Scott's latest message once again.

"Anderson and Clark are back from their assignment. They're running the first of the searches now. The historic ones are slow, and there are a lot of regions to collate. They should be done by five a.m. at the latest, and I'll send the results through asap. You get some rest. By morning, hopefully there will be work to do."

Nothing more she could do.

At that moment, Leblanc walked in.

Katie glanced up, pleased to see him. He looked tired from the drive through the dark, snowy, testing conditions, and he also looked annoyed that the lead hadn't panned out.

"What happened out there?" she asked, hoping he could elaborate on the short message he'd sent.

"The guy was innocent. The girl was angry that he'd told her to move her car, and looking to get the police after him. Wrong place, wrong time for us. A two-hour detour there and back, for nothing." He grimaced ruefully.

"I feel worried this guy is still out there," Katie said.

She'd ordered food already as the kitchen was closing early on this quiet, winter night. Now, the waitress arrived with two large bowls of rich beef stew, with slices of fresh bread.

"Thank you," Leblanc said gratefully.

Having not thought about food all day, Katie suddenly realized how hungry she was.

"I hope tomorrow brings results," she said. "We need a bigger overview of this. I hope something turns up in the search the task force is doing."

Leblanc nodded, as he ladled up a big spoonful of stew and began to eat.

"I'm sure it will," he said, sounding more confident than Katie felt.

Katie couldn't shake the fear that the killer was out there. Driving, waiting, planning. A man they didn't know and hadn't even gotten close to. A shadowy figure whose agenda she couldn't figure out. She had an uneasy feeling there was something important about him that she didn't know, but needed to.

By tomorrow, she hoped it would be clearer.

She spooned a mouthful of stew into her mouth and savored the rich, hearty taste. Comfort food was at least some consolation, at the end of a long, cold, and unrewarding day. The stew was hot and filling. It tasted delicious.

The only thing that could make it taste better, Katie acknowledged, would be to eat it after this case had been successfully concluded.

She ate fast, needing to sate her hunger and also realizing how tired she was becoming. The entire day had been exhausting. This case felt emotionally draining.

Hungrily, she spooned up the last mouthful.

"I guess we should get some rest," she said. "If these results will be ready early, let's meet at six a.m.? Look over what we have and see if any new leads result from it?"

Leblanc nodded. "Good idea."

Katie headed upstairs to her room. It was a small, cozy room that was warmly decorated in shades of red and blue, with a window overlooking the frozen street below, and thick red curtains to blot out that cold, icy vista.

She showered in the postage-stamp sized bathroom and she climbed into bed.

The bed was soft and comfortable. But Katie's mind was racing.

She'd felt so tired as she'd finished her meal downstairs. Now, her mind was full of worries. Thoughts of her sister dominated. She always got nightmares on a case, and she feared they would be worse this time. She worried that if she fell asleep, she'd be transported straight to Gabriel Rath's lair, that existed in her imagination and maybe also elsewhere. She might see her sister - afraid and alone, captured and held, just as Sherrie had been.

Katie didn't want to fall asleep and face that. She turned and twisted, trying to get herself comfortable. She didn't want to fall asleep; she wanted to stay awake and ensure that she didn't have an anxiety dream.

But her mind was active.

She'd been too tense, too busy, too worried, too scared, and too distracted to let her mind wander. But now, she couldn't sleep, even though she was so tired.

As she lay there, still and tense, she heard a movement in the room. She'd locked the door. But somebody had managed to get in.

Her eyes flew open, and she sat up. In the shadows, she could make out a shape. It was a man.

She recognized him at once.

Rath.

The tall, bearded man stood at the side of her bed. He held a knife. He was smiling.

"Where is your sister?" he asked softly. Katie felt a jolt of fear.

"You can tell me, you know. Where is your sister?" He moved closer. Katie's heart pounded with fear.

"Tell me where Josie is," he insisted. "I know you know. I will torment you until you tell."

Katie wanted to scream at him to go away, but found she couldn't speak. Terror had seized her. Her mouth was dry. She tried to swallow, but she couldn't. She could feel his presence filling the room. He loomed over her like a giant in the shadows.

"Where is she? It's your last chance to tell me," he decided.

Katie moved suddenly - to the edge of the bed, and then she was up and running. She ran for the door, but she couldn't make it. The door was too far away for her to reach, it was hundreds of yards away, and she started to scream in terror.

Behind her, the knife flashed.

"Tell me now, or I'll take you instead," he threatened, his voice soft and sibilant, menacing. He loomed over her, a giant figure that she could not escape.

And then Rath looked up, angry and distracted, because someone was knocking at the door. Pounding on the wood.

With an evil laugh, he strode to the window, disappearing easily through it. Katie erupted from her nightmare, sitting up, gasping in a huge breath. The dream was gone. Rath had melted away.

But the knocking - that was still there. She heard it again. She climbed out of bed, feeling totally spooked from that awful, vivid dream.

"Who is it?" she whispered, padding over the carpet to the door.

"It's me," Leblanc replied.

"What is it? Is everything alright?" Katie unlocked the door.

Leblanc was standing outside. She saw he was dressed for bed. He was in a black dressing gown.

"I know you - you have nightmares when we are on cases. I thought I heard you shouting. I wondered if you wanted company," he whispered.

Katie knew, with a sudden and surprising warmth in her stomach, that this wasn't what he was asking. It wasn't all.

Last time they had been on a case, she'd gone to his room after a bad dream. He'd held her and they had slept. But this time - this time, she knew that if she let him in, it would be more. He wanted more. She also did, but was she ready?

There was no doubt it would go further.

She felt the attraction between them. She felt his gaze on her. Sensed the warmth of his skin and the expression tautening the lean planes of his face.

This was more than just companionship. Was she ready?

"What do you think?" Leblanc asked softly.

Katie thought about her sister. She thought about the case. She thought about how she wanted to feel his arms around her.

"Yes," she said, opening the door wider.

Leblanc's eyes met hers, and she felt a jolt of sensation in her belly.

Katie wanted this, she wanted to let him in, to hold him close, to allow him to touch her. She wanted to have honesty between them, and to be close to this man, whom she trusted with her life.

She could not deny it any longer.

But she knew, even as she stepped forward into his arms and the door closed behind him, that it was most likely a bad idea. It was a complication they shouldn't look for and couldn't afford.

She didn't care. She was falling for Leblanc, and was all out of will power to say no. And maybe yes was the right decision. As long as she could cope with the emotional weight that this would add to their partnership.

CHAPTER NINETEEN

It was early morning, a gray, dull day on the East Coast.

FBI Special Agent Goodman strode into the meeting room. The three men he was due to meet with were already there. The first, gray-haired Richards, was a fellow FBI director from the head office. Another, Mercer, was from the U.S. Department of Defense. Usually, Goodman found him arrogant. And the final delegate, Cooper, was a RCMP Deputy Commissioner, who had flown in early to attend this meeting. He looked anxious.

"Morning, gentlemen," Goodman said, taking his seat at the head of the oaken table in the plush, quiet meeting room.

It was here, in this hushed environment, that so much of what happened at street level, on the ground, was decided.

Today, the meeting was an unusual one. For the first time, they were discussing a relatively new unit.

"I'd like to open this meeting," Goodman said. "We're going to speak about the cross-border task force that's been operating the last few months on and around the US-Canada border."

"What's the update on that?" Mercer asked, clicking through his tablet, as if there were more important things for him to focus his attention on.

"It's interesting," Goodman nodded. "It was a joint effort. The FBI has a long-standing agreement with the RCMP to share intelligence, and we have a history of strong support for their efforts in Canada. They are our international partners in this case."

"The operation is not brand new," Richards added.

"No, it isn't. The task force has been operational for a few months now. I've been in touch with the RCMP Commissioner about that. In this period, they've had some surprising successes, and in this folder, I have the details of those. We've also had some problems with the Canadian end of the operation, and a few unexpected costs on both sides, because the unit utilizes other police resources and does not have any vehicles, helicopters, or other equipment of its own. But mainly, we've had resistance from three key individuals in three of the U.S. states along the border. Those states are named in the report I've compiled."

"What do they say?" Richards asked.

"They say that the task force is causing interference with their own investigations. That there's an unnecessary overlap and duplication of resources."

Goodman had the attention of the other three, who were focused on him, listening carefully, ready to hear what he had to say.

"Anything else?" Cooper asked. "We need to handle these problems, right?"

"They've voiced serious concerns that the task force is without any direction. They are concerned that it is operating without sufficient oversight, and that it could cause serious diplomatic problems down the line – they've said they don't want to create a potential political minefield."

"I'm glad you've brought this to our attention," Cooper said. "I know that the RCMP is working well with the task force, so I'm sorry to hear there are problems from the U.S. side. That's clearly where they originate."

Mercer snorted, looking offended at his words.

"Where do we go from here?" Richards asked.

"I have been advised we should probably shut down the operation in the next month," Goodman said, voicing the words reluctantly.

"But it's been highly effective," Richards argued, frowning. "I know a couple of the agents personally who are part of it. They're very good, very experienced. And they've got an excellent solve rate. Crime in that area has always been problematic due to its cross border nature. There are a number of politicians who have given me very positive feedback on the results."

"What's the nature of the problem?" Cooper asked, sounding worried.

"There isn't one," Richards argued. "I'm all for shutting down a task force if it's ineffective, but I don't think that this is. It's a highly dedicated unit, and they're getting results, solving serious crimes - one of the best solve rates in the country. I think we should leave it alone."

"We can't leave it alone." Goodman shook his head. "It's a sensitive situation. You have to remember the job of this task force is to fight crime in order to protect both sides. However, they're not always working with our diplomatic goals in mind. We don't want any international problems, and we don't want to expose our officials to any potential conflicts of interest."

There was a pause as each of these men considered the arguments. Not only the facts, but also the political ramifications. In politics, things were seldom simple or straightforward.

Some things could not be said, but only implied. Goodman knew that the individuals complaining about this were all very politically ambitious. And behind them was somebody else. He knew where the complaints and pressure originated from. And he knew which powerful individual wanted the task force removed for political reasons that related to their own goals.

But he couldn't say a word about that. All he was empowered to do was discuss the facts and arguments presented at this meeting.

"I've got the figures in front of me," Cooper added. "They're better - far better - than anything else we have. And we have many other task forces that have been running for years, with far more resources and far more people allocated."

"I'm sure we can consider it in light of the successes they've had," Richards said. "What do you think, sir?" he asked, knowing that it was Mercer's turn to chime in.

"I'm all for keeping it viable if it's effective, but it sounds as if it's creating too many problems," Mercer said dubiously.

The men around the table exchanged glances, thinking about the implications of those facts.

"The task force is effective," Richards said.

"Why shut it down?" Cooper asked in pleading tones. "This will be a massive blow for the RCMP, and the people on our side of the border."

"Shutting it down is the recommendation I've received," Goodman said.

"What reason would you give for shutting it down?" Richards challenged.

"It goes down to the question of oversight and control," Goodman explained. "We want to be sure that the unit is working in the interests of everyone, and unfortunately from the negative feedback I have received, that does not seem to be possible. If we have political opposition to it, it creates an immediate problem."

"If you did shut it down, would you replace it?" Cooper asked.

"The government officials who've engaged with me have discussed a new unit," Goodman explained. "They won't have the same freedom to operate. It'll be a more traditional unit, working under more stringent controls."

"There's no point in keeping a unit if we can't ensure its independence," Cooper said, almost to himself. "That would make it ineffective."

"Look, the police did a good job before this task force was created," Richards said, always one to acknowledge both sides with the wisdom of his experience. "But I don't think we should be making any rash decisions."

"After speaking to you all, and reading through the report, my feeling is also that it would be unwise to rush into a decision," Goodman said. "I think we must explain to the individuals who have expressed their concerns that we are scrutinizing the unit and that we will make a formal announcement in a few more weeks after we've analyzed all the input."

"The announcement should come from the joint FBI-RCMP press offices," Richards added. "That will make it clear that it's been approved."

"Agreed," Goodman nodded.

"We need this unit," Cooper insisted. "I don't want to see it shut down."

Mercer sighed, thumping the table with his hands. "There are more important things to focus on than this. This task force is relatively new, and it's tiny. We managed for years without it. I don't see that it's such a big issue if it shuts down."

Cooper glared at him, but said nothing.

"I think we've all had our say now. Thank you for your help," Goodman said, shaking hands with each of them. "I value your input, and we'll meet again soon when we finalize the next step," he added, and then he ushered them out of the room.

Goodman stood up and walked over to the window, gazing out over the city. He felt uneasy about this.

The results of the task force had been excellent. More than any of them realized, he thought - as he gazed out over the city, his hands clasped behind his back.

Political agendas had destroyed better units before now, and he knew there was only so much pushback that he could apply.

He decided that he would not make the decision - yet. He'd gotten the feedback he needed.

He'd table the final decision for the next end-of-month meeting. There was no rush.

Deep down, despite the politics, he was at heart a detective himself who understood the importance of solving crimes.

He didn't want to see the unit closed. But he didn't know if his own opinion and belief would be enough to sway the implacable might of political agendas, if they decided against it.

CHAPTER TWENTY

Katie woke from a deep, dreamless sleep. Memories surfaced in her mind of what had happened between them. She'd fallen asleep in Leblanc's arms. It had felt right. More than right. She'd been comforted, she'd felt safe and content and fulfilled.

But now, it was morning, and she needed to urgently put the emotions and memories aside.

In fact, it had been the sound of the door closing softly behind Leblanc that had woken her and she knew he felt the same way, that it was time to get to work, and that what had happened last night must not affect the dynamic of today.

Emotional entanglement would not help them now as they tracked down this rogue killer.

But even so, as she headed for the shower, she couldn't help a smile, a feeling of warmth, as she remembered what had happened between them. A space in her heart, that had been walled off for so long, finally felt as if it was alive again.

But she knew it must not affect their work. Imagine if the affair between them smeared the unit's reputation?

Nobody should know about this yet, Katie resolved, guessing that Leblanc felt exactly the same. For now, this needed to be their secret.

Heading to the bathroom, Katie showered quickly. She got dressed, packed her things, and headed downstairs to the hotel's lounge.

There, Leblanc was organizing coffee and her heart jumped as she saw him. Memories surged again, despite her efforts to suppress them. Good memories. The kind she wanted to savor forever. The touch of his lips and hands. The sound of his breathing and the feel of his body against hers.

For so long, Katie had resisted getting involved with anyone. She hadn't trusted enough. But she trusted him.

"Coffee?" Leblanc asked, with a quirk of his mouth that told her he shared her thoughts, but like her, was keeping them private. She appreciated that.

The aroma of the coffee was sweet and rich, cutting through the last of her tiredness.

They sat down together at one of the tables and got ready to see what the night's research had brought.

"I hope we find something," Katie said. "I really hope we do."

As she scanned the list, Katie saw to her surprise that there was a definite spike in missing person cases over the past few months.

Since the beginning of the year, a total of seven women, ranging in age from twenty-one to thirty-five, had been reported missing. Two of them had gone missing from nearby in The Pas, two from Winnipeg, and the other three from smaller towns further north.

The first case from the list had been reported to the RCMP on January 20th, from The Pas.

The second case had been reported on February 2nd to the Winnipeg police. And from there, there were others.

Katie felt a chill. Once you started pulling the threads together, she thought the pattern was unmistakable.

"This is very interesting," she heard Leblanc murmur and knew that his investigator's mind was as intrigued by this as hers was.

Was this abnormal? Had a similar spike occurred previously?

"We need to look at the previous years. Do a comparison," Katie said.

"Yes. Let's do that. It will be important," Leblanc agreed.

Katie looked back over the past records, scrolling through the archives that the task force had compiled during the night.

"Now this is interesting," she said. "Only two women were reported missing in Manitoba during the whole of last year. And one was subsequently found unharmed."

"The year before, two. One was found alive, one found dead," Leblanc said. "And the year before that, one, a runaway who was discovered in Vancouver."

"So this is definitely unusual," Katie said. "The statistics are clear. What we are seeing this year is a massive spike in the disappearances of females. But because the province is so huge and these disappearances have occurred over such a wide area, it's not been picked up until now."

"Also, none have been found," Leblanc said.

"Absolutely."

An uneasy tingle of anxiety began to worm its way into Katie's consciousness. She tried to dismiss it, but it wouldn't go away.

They were silent a while and Katie found her thoughts going again to Sherrie's account of what the killer had said.

In this vast landscape it would be easy to dump a body in a place it would never be found, or else might only be found months later, nothing more than bones.

But why had the killer suddenly started targeting women? Katie wondered. Why had he started hunting out here in this lonely expanse? What had triggered these suspected kills?

"One thing is certain. He's not going to stop," Leblanc said.

"I agree. He's not going to stop until we stop him," Katie acknowledged. "But this shows me that he started this year. So, something happened. He came here, he moved here, or he was triggered to begin killing women in a wide area. And that already gives us some more pointers."

They were quiet for a moment, thinking about what these new insights offered.

"We need to do some digging," Katie said after a pause. "We need to try to establish a link, and see if we can find anything that will help us narrow down who he is. At least now we have more common factors. Perhaps we can get evidence that can point us to him more clearly."

"We need to do that," Leblanc said.

Katie gulped her coffee and stood up. Time to start.

"There are two women reported missing in this town, right here. That seems to be a good starting point. We might get more details on the circumstances. We could each do interviews about one."

The two women were Pamela South, who disappeared in February, and Kelsey Dupont, who was reported missing two weeks ago. Both had close connections in The Pas. Pamela's mother lived here, and Kelsey had been sharing a house with family friends.

"Okay. Here are the phone numbers," Katie said, and she handed over the sheets of paper where she'd written down the information.

Leblanc nodded.

"Shall I go to Pamela's family, you go to Kelsey's?" Katie asked.

"Let's do that," Leblanc said.

They packed their equipment away, and left the hotel.

It was another icy day, Katie realized, stepping outside. Even colder than yesterday. Snowflakes were swirling in the air, which had a frigid bite to it.

Katie felt hopeful, but apprehensive, about what the day would bring.

She was very aware that the killer could already have taken another victim, one who had not yet been reported missing.

Uneasily, she realized she was waiting for the call she dreaded, and hoped that she'd be able to get a lead on him before this happened, from Pamela South's family.

CHAPTER TWENTY ONE

Katie walked up to the modest single-story home with a tiny, snow-covered yard, hoping that Cheryl South, Pamela's mother, would provide clues to take this investigation further. She had called ahead to introduce herself, not wanting to provide a moment's worry or worse still, any false hope, by appearing unannounced on her doorstep at such a time.

Something was happening. Somehow, these women were disappearing. And she needed to find out who was taking them, and how the killer was going about his deadly business.

When Cheryl opened the door, Katie immediately sensed the worry and sadness emanating from her. She was a petite woman, with a pale face and tired, red eyes.

"Come in," Cheryl said softly. "It's so kind of you to come see me."

Katie steeled herself for the ordeal ahead, and prepared to do whatever she could to help this woman who had lost her daughter – forever, she feared.

"Thank you for seeing me at such short notice," she said. "I do appreciate it."

"Let's go into the kitchen," Cheryl said.

The house was not big, but it was warm and comfortable. The open plan kitchen and dining room area was neat and tidy, and there was a pot of coffee brewing on the stove.

Katie sat down, taking in the homey touches that Cheryl had added to the room. Photographs of Pamela were placed here and there, her high school diploma proudly displayed on the wall. Proof of hope, more than a month after her daughter's disappearance. It wrenched Katie's heart. Pamela's mother had been through an experience that would leave scars. And every day that passed with no news would also add to those scars.

"Would you like some coffee?" Cheryl asked, looking at her wanly.

"Yes, please," Katie said. "I hope you don't mind if I ask you a few questions?"

"No, no. I know you have to do that. Please have a seat," Cheryl said.

Sitting down, Katie saw a scrapbook was open on the table, filled with photos of Pamela as a child, and more recent ones of her as a young woman.

"It's been so hard," Cheryl said.

"I can imagine," Katie said, and her heart ached for this woman.

"Pamela was my only child," Cheryl said. "I called the police. I did what I was supposed to do. But at the start, they said it was likely she ran away. She'd done that before, you see."

"What did you think?" Katie asked.

"I knew she hadn't run away. But she was wanting to go south to visit a friend. She didn't have a car. She used to hitchhike."

"You think she would have done that?" Katie realized now that there was a definite link to be picked up. Had both these local victims hitchhiked? She was beginning to think so.

"She'd done it before. I disapproved of it, so she didn't tell us until she was back, most times. I told her to wait until she could get a ride with someone we knew but she was an impatient girl."

Katie could see the sadness in Cheryl's eyes.

"So you don't think she would have listened to you?"

"She was young and flighty. We all make mistakes when we're young and the world is open in front of us. She was very independent."

"Would you say she was troubled?" Katie asked.

"Not really," Cheryl said thoughtfully. "She was just on a rebellious streak. Whatever I told her to do, she'd choose the opposite."

"Do you know if she took anything with her when she left?" Katie asked.

"Just her purse and a small travel bag. I worked out a few clothes were missing. She took her phone but it was never found. We tried to trace it, but it was an old model, and we found it was turned off."

"What time of day did she disappear?"

"In the morning. Early on a Saturday morning. That's also what made me think she was planning on hitching. She probably wanted to be in Winnipeg before it got dark." Cheryl smiled sadly. "She was so independent. Too independent. She was young and she wasn't aware of danger."

"At that age, who is?" Katie agreed sadly.

At sixteen, she'd been even less aware.

"I tried so hard to do my best for her but when I did, she would rebel. I still think maybe she will come home. Maybe she was angry with us for some reason and decided not to tell us she was going. But then I look at her social media. I do that daily. And she hasn't updated it. She always used to do that, every day. So deep down, I think she's gone."

She sighed.

Katie felt deep sympathy for her. She was going through exactly what Katie's own parents had to endure with Josie's disappearance.

It was so hard to accept that somebody could vanish from your life and never come back.

It strengthened her resolve to get to the bottom of what was going on. Even if it was too late for Pamela, which she suspected it was, at least she could provide closure, and an end to worry and false hope for her mother.

"Thank you for your time," she said. "I hope we can get answers for you. What you've said has been very helpful."

She stood up and left. As she walked out, she thought about what Cheryl had said. Heartbreaking as the visit had been, she had finally picked up on a possible common thread, which was that both of the victims might have been hitchhiking. And that in turn opened up a clearer line of thinking as to who might be responsible for abducting them. She wondered how Leblanc's interview had gone, and hoped that he had gotten similar feedback, because this would guide them further onto this path. She decided to call him as soon as she was in the car.

Stepping outside, Katie saw the roads had been cleared, but there was still a layer of ice on the ground, and slushy snow on the road. More bad weather was building, with gray clouds looming.

As she reached her car, her phone rang, and she saw it was Scott on the line.

Katie had a very bad feeling about this. She didn't even want to take this call. She feared that what she had been dreading had happened. Ever since this case began, she'd known deep down that there would be news of more victims.

She felt certain that this was why Scott was calling now.

The only question in her mind, as she picked up, was whether this news would relate to one of the women they already knew about.

Or whether it would be somebody new, that might possibly provide a more recent lead to the identity of the killer.

CHAPTER TWENTY TWO

Leblanc walked into the coffee shop where the Maidstone family, who owned the house where Kelsey had lived and were good friends of hers, had agreed to meet him. They lived a few miles out of town, and both worked in town. This meeting would save them all time.

Leblanc thought that perhaps they also didn't want him intruding into their private space. He respected that. Whatever was easiest for them at such a difficult time, he was glad to go along with.

He spotted them as soon as he walked into the stark, but warm, coffee shop on the corner of a main street in the town center. They were both wearing dark jackets, sitting close, unsmiling.

Mrs. Maidstone looked up, frowning slightly.

"Detective Leblanc," he said.

"Mr. and Mrs. Maidstone," she introduced them. "We are close family friends of Kelsey's mother, who lives in Vancouver. We are pretty much shattered by this. She was here for a gap year, doing some long-distance courses. With this having happened, we feel we failed her parents."

Leblanc sat down across from the two of them. He could see they were both feeling stressed and traumatized over what had happened. He could only guess at how complex and heartbreaking it had been to lose a close family friend under these circumstances.

"Thank you for agreeing to speak to me," he said.

"I can't take much time away from work," Mr. Maidstone said. "With what's happened over the past months, I've used up all my leave, trying to search for her and following up on what we've been told. I work for an electrician and this time of year is always busy, with it being so cold. The company has been accommodating but in the end, bills have to be paid," he said tiredly.

"I'll be as quick as I can," Leblanc said, feeling doubly sympathetic toward their predicament.

"Kelsey went missing at the end of January, correct?"

"Yes, that's right," Mrs. Maidstone said.

"Do you know the circumstances?"

"She wanted to go to a festival in a small town called Woodlands, which is about two hundred miles away from here, going north," Mrs.

Maidstone explained. "She had a couple of friends there, and there was a winter music festival. We thought she'd have to cancel her plans as she had a small car, but it broke down and she had no other way of getting there. Unfortunately, we couldn't take her. My husband was on a twelve-hour shift, and I work in a doctor's office, and had to man the reception."

"So what happened?"

Mrs. Maidstone sighed. "She messaged me to say she had made a plan. And that was the last we heard of her."

"Did she tell you what the plan was?" Leblanc asked.

"No," Mrs. Maidstone said. "I texted her back and asked, but I didn't get a reply."

"Except someone saw her," Mr. Maidstone added.

"Is that so?" Leblanc asked.

"It was one of our neighbors. They said they saw her standing by the side of the main road and it looked like she was hitchhiking."

"So she tried to hitch a ride up there?"

"Yes. They were going the opposite way and thought nothing of it. They have a son who hitchhikes occasionally. I don't think they realized she was trying to go so far. They told us the next day that they'd seen her there."

"So it doesn't sound like she ever made it to the festival."

"No," Mr. Maidstone said. "We checked with her friends, and that was confirmed. Nobody saw her at the festival. She messaged them to say she thought she'd be able to get there, but never arrived."

"We never heard back from her after that. Of course, we tried calling her phone, but it was switched off. The police were very good, they followed up, I think they did everything they could. Her mother flew out here and spent a few days looking. We did everything we could, but it was as if she'd simply vanished," Mrs. Maidstone said.

"Did she go off on her own often?"

"No," Mrs. Maidstone shook her head. "It was very unusual for her and I don't know if she'd even hitchhiked before. Not that I know of, of course. She could have done it with friends, and not told me. We tried not to intrude too much on her privacy, because she was basically here to live her own life and be more independent, even though she was also a family friend."

"She was usually a responsible girl," Mr. Maidstone said. "It was this damned festival that made her determined to get away. If I'd known she was so keen to attend, we could have made a plan. She probably decided on impulse."

Leblanc noted that they were speaking of her in the past tense. He guessed that they had decided to accept the most likely scenario, painful as it was, which was that their young friend was no longer alive.

Leblanc felt terrible as he watched them, and although his attention was keenly focused on them, he couldn't help a fleeting thought that this was what it had been like for Katie's parents. She had been through this exact same trauma, with her missing twin.

No wonder it had scarred her so deeply, he thought, with a flare of sympathy for the pain in their faces.

"I think she was picked up by the wrong person. She was an innocent girl. Young. In her early twenties. She didn't know how evil people can be," Mrs. Maidstone explained.

"So you feel this was a well-meaning adventure that ended in tragedy?"

"Yes," Mr. Maidstone said. "If you want my opinion, she got in the wrong car. If she had told me about the plan, I would have warned her about that. Someone she didn't know might have approached her with ulterior motives."

"If I ever get hold of that monster, his time here is over," Mrs. Maidstone threatened, and Leblanc could see the fury in her eyes.

"I hope that we will find this person soon, and that he is punished to the full might of the law," Leblanc agreed, knowing that the words were not enough, but yet they were all he could offer them. Not wanting to delay them, he got up.

"Thank you for your time," he said.

At least he knew they had a starting point.

Kelsey had been hitchhiking and something must have gone wrong. But this did create a common thread and that gave them a glimmer of light into the direction they needed to take.

Both Kelsey and Sherrie could have been hitching a ride and perhaps the same person had picked them up. It was also worth noting that they had both been looking to travel long distances.

What he didn't know was what was happening after they were picked up. Why had Sherrie had those injuries. What was this guy doing? Had he been picking them up, and then things had turned bad? Or was he a psychopath, who used this as an opportunity to seek out and then murder young women on the road?

Leblanc was leaning toward the second explanation as being the more likely.

He would need to pass the information along to the RCMP departments immediately. He knew he had to share this new information with them so that they could warn the public. They couldn't keep this under wraps. Even though it would cause panic, the awareness would mean that, potentially, people could make different decisions and lives could be saved.

Heading for his car, Leblanc heard his phone ring.

It was Katie.

As soon as he picked up, he heard in her voice that something had happened.

"I just got a call from Scott," she explained. "They've found another body, and suspect that it's the work of this killer."

"Where?" Leblanc asked.

"It was near a frozen lake, close to the main road, about an hour's drive north of here. Where do you want to meet? From what Scott said, this is a recent kill. She was definitely murdered. There might be something we can pick up from the scene."

Leblanc felt anxiety flare inside him. Another victim had died. They'd been unable to prevent it, and too slow.

All they could hope for was that this more recent kill could provide new information.

"Let's meet at the RCMP department, and drive together from there," he said.

CHAPTER TWENTY THREE

When Katie climbed out of the car at the crime scene, her first impression was how isolated this area was.

A ribbon of tarmac, encroached by snow, wound its way through silent, white hills. The sky loomed overhead, dark and threatening with more snow to come.

Nearby was a frozen lake, with thick ice around it, and no buildings or lights nearby. There was a dark forest on the other side of the lake, which was to her left.

There was a frosty silence and the wind was lashing at her face with tiny ice daggers.

The only splash of color in this austere landscape was the flashing lights and the garish looking crime scene tape that demarcated where the body was found.

Katie headed over, with Leblanc a silent presence behind her, not wanting to look, but knowing she had to see.

The first person she saw was clearly the man who had found the body.

The tall man, in his sixties, was standing with an RCMP officer and turned to Katie and Leblanc, looking stressed. He still seemed to be in a state of shock, ready to tell his story to whoever would listen.

"I got out of the car for a pee, and then my drugstore bag fell out of the car and the wind took it. I chased after it into the hills, and as I walked, I saw this leg. A leg, sticking out from a snowdrift. I couldn't believe it. I still can't. How could this happen? Here, in such a quiet part of the world?"

He sounded incredulous and sad.

"What kind of a place is this? I have lived here all my life, I have never felt unsafe before, but this is just too much." He was speaking quickly, emotion coloring his voice and making it waver.

"I know you feel that way," the officer said, and Katie could tell he was trying to soothe him by responding kindly and with empathy. "This must be very distressing."

Having heard his account and offered her sympathy, Katie walked over to the crime scene tape where the body lay.

She stared down at a tall woman in her late twenties. Her hair was a dull blonde, and her eyes were wide.

She was lying in the snow, wearing jeans and a sweater, half-covered by an icy drift. The pathologist was at work already, wearing PPE over his heavy parka, his eyes focused above his mask.

"Is this where she was found?" Katie asked.

"Yes," the officer said in a low voice.

"Do we have an ID for her?"

"Lizanne Bright. She had ID in her pocket. We're following up now and trying to locate her next of kin."

"And when was she found?"

"We got the call about an hour ago. We traveled to the scene immediately. The pathologist, Dr. Simms, got here before us."

Dr. Simms glanced up.

"This is a recent death. Probably, she was killed less than twelve hours ago. There's no sign of the body being moved, so I guess she was killed right here. When I arrived there was evidence of footprints, but they were little more than indentations, mostly obscured by this blowing wind, on top of loose snow. There wasn't enough for us to analyze or draw any conclusions."

"What is the cause of death?" Katie asked the pathologist.

"She was shot, in the back. Once. A single shot, dead center. It went straight through her heart, and was fatal. But what's interesting is that she has something on her neck here."

He pointed to the faint mark on the pale, lifeless flesh, and Katie looked closer.

"That's a mark from a taser, surely?" she said, recognizing it, feeling surprised.

"Yes. It looks very clear to me. Two burn marks. And there are another two on the other side of her neck. I would imagine she was tasered, and then shot. Then left here in the cold."

"Did she have any visible defensive wounds?" Katie asked.

"A couple of grazes on her arms, but nothing deep enough to be serious," the pathologist replied.

"Did you find anything else on the scene?" she asked the officer.

"We haven't had a chance to do a search for other evidence yet. We have to wait for that until the pathologist is done," he said.

The wind picked up then, sending a chill through Katie, and she shivered. This was a horrific scenario to imagine. She had no idea what type of person would be capable of doing such a thing. Why?

How could she get into their mind, and get closer to them, and try to pinpoint who they were? All she had were a series of violent and random actions that represented only a small part of the puzzle. They didn't know enough.

Katie looked back at the body, feeling a sense of sadness coming over her.

She felt certain this was what had happened to the other victims. In remote areas, wild animals would have made short work of these dumped bodies, leaving few traces.

"I'll need to do a full postmortem on the body, once we get her back to the pathology office," the pathologist said. "I might not be able to tell you too much more, but I will certainly let you know if anything else of significance is found."

Katie nodded. She didn't want to think about the body being taken away just yet. She still wanted to take in the scene, and try to gain some insight from it.

This killer was operating in remote areas. He was leaving bodies where they might never be discovered. The fact that this body was found so fast had been no more than a lucky coincidence, but not lucky enough. They needed to know more.

"Any tire tracks? Any signs of the vehicle stopping that dumped her?" Katie asked.

"With the snow and the wind, not enough. It's clear that a few vehicles have passed this way within the past couple of hours," the officer said.

"Any cameras along this route?"

"No. The closest camera would be on the highway, and that's a good few miles away."

Katie sighed, feeling frustrated. When were they going to get a break in the case? How were they going to figure out why the killer was doing this?

She visualized him as a cold-minded man, laughing at their confusion and distress. He could kill, and get away with it. And he was probably still out there, moving along the highways, searching for more victims.

But she had the feeling there was more to it. There must be a reason behind these kills. What was he doing it for? What was going through his mind as he carried out the abductions, knowing that in the end, he was going to taser and shoot his captives? Katie stared at the crime scene, feeling a sense of helplessness. She wanted to be able to make sense of this, to be able to stop this murderer, but she had no idea how to do it.

The questions were piling up, and she had no answers.

"We need to map out where the two bodies were found, and where the other women have gone missing," Leblanc said. "Perhaps when we look at the locations, we can see some kind of a pattern to it."

"That's a good idea," Katie said. "Now that we have more information, we can do that immediately."

"The police in Winnipeg have just visited her parents, to break the news of her death," the officer said. "Apparently she was in trouble with them. She left home yesterday morning, and they think she was trying to hitchhike up to a friend who lives in one of the northern mining communities. They're obviously devastated but were able to call the friend and confirm that she'd contacted them to say she'd try and get there."

Katie raised her eyebrows.

"So this was yet another victim taken in this area of the number 10 highway?"

"Looks like it," Leblanc confirmed.

"It has to be a serial. It has to. And now, we know where he's operating. We know the area. It can lead us to him, I know it can," Katie insisted. "It's surely someone who's driving this route, back and forth. Who's been driving it all winter. So we're looking for a winter-specific occupation."

"A transport driver? Or even a snowplow driver?" Leblanc's face lit up with excitement as he followed her train of thought.

CHAPTER TWENTY FOUR

As Katie and Leblanc drove, Katie was thinking frantically about this crime, and how they could narrow down possibilities to get them closer to the answer they needed.

"What if Lizanne's friend knew more about where she was?" she asked. "If you were hitchhiking, trying to get to a friend, wouldn't you give progress reports en route?"

Leblanc shrugged. "I guess it would depend on if you had the wi-fi available to do it."

"According to the information in this report, the friend is a couple of hundred miles north of The Pas, and her name is Samantha Sheridan. Her husband works for one of the mines."

"Have the police not spoken to her yet?"

"I see from this report that they spoke to her briefly, and reported her as being very upset. I don't think they got a lot of coherent information from her, but perhaps now that she's had some more time, she'll be ready to talk. It's too far to drive. Let's call her when we get to the RCMP."

They were heading for the closest RCMP department, which was in a small town north of The Pas, called Windermere. There, Katie hoped, they could find a desk, log onto the systems, and do some more research.

Thinking out loud, Katie summarized what they had so far.

"Whoever this killer is, he's capturing the women, and transporting them for some distance. Why? What does this link to? What's going on in his mind? We have to understand this, if we're going to find him."

Leblanc shook his head. "Getting into the minds of these guys is your forte. Mine is research. So maybe we should start there. Let's start with the snowplows as they would be driving a demarcated route, and be on the road a lot of the time. We can look at the records of the snowplow drivers in this province. Who is hired? What are the parameters? We need to find out more about it, and to do that, we probably need to speak to someone in the local government."

Katie felt as if they had narrowed the prospects down, but there were still so many directions it could take.

They were pulling up outside the Windermere RCMP department. It was a small, modest building in a town that felt low and snow-blown, flanked by dark woods.

"Let me handle that," Leblanc said. "My department. Routine research."

Katie parked, and he climbed out of the car and hurried into the police department. By the time she followed him, he was already speaking on the phone.

Katie felt grateful for his local knowledge. Having grown up in Canada, and spent the past couple of years back home again after his time in Paris, he would know more about the internal workings of the province than she would. She felt grateful for his support in this area.

She wasn't quite sure what the relationship was between them. She was still preparing herself for what came next.

And in between wondering what would play out there, she couldn't help feeling a terrible guilt about this case. Women were being abducted. It brought back her past so intensely.

She'd had nightmares wondering if Josie had been somehow grabbed and taken. It had haunted her for years.

Now, the stark reality was that someone was at work, abducting these women. And if she didn't find out why, there might be many more fatalities.

She walked over to the department's front desk, introducing themselves.

"Agent Winter and Detective Leblanc. We're investigating a string of crimes in this area. May we work in your back office?" she asked the officer in attendance.

"Sure," he nodded, waving them through.

Katie headed through to the back office. Still on the phone, Leblanc followed.

She opened her laptop, accessed the case documents, and a minute later, was dialing Samantha's number.

A woman answered, sounding stressed.

"Samantha here," she said.

"Samantha, it's Katie Winter here. We're investigating Lizanne's death."

Samantha burst into tears, forcing Katie to wait a minute before continuing.

"I'm so sorry," she said.

"I can understand how difficult this is," Katie sympathized. "But I wondered if you had received any communication from Lizanne while she was on her way. Perhaps she told you her location, or said she was looking for a ride somewhere?"

There was a pause.

"Yes, she did give me an update. She sent me a message to call her, and when I called, she said she was at a truck stop somewhere north of Winnipeg. The guy she'd been driving with lived in that town so he couldn't take her further, I think. I wish I could remember where she said it was. She did mention the name. I'll look at a map and see if anything sounds familiar. If I remember, can I call you back?"

"Please," Katie said.

Frustratingly, this wasn't going to get them any further for now. Not unless Samantha remembered more.

But what was important is that she'd been on the highway, the number 10 highway, looking for a ride. Katie felt surer than ever that this was the killer's hunting ground.

Leblanc was still on the phone to his contact, and Katie hoped that he would get somewhere. He spoke for a few more moments and then cut the call.

"Okay. I got through to the right person. All the provincial highways are staffed by registered snowplow drivers and they are sending me a list. We can check them off against the criminal database. They said they check too, but off the record, he said not as thoroughly as they should. It's seasonal work and there's often a shortage of workers."

"Yes, that makes sense," Katie said.

"There are also those who are privately employed to do work in more local areas, and they don't have a say over that. But we agreed that for one of those drivers to be driving an actual snowplow up and down highway 10, would be basically impossible. So for someone to cover this territory, we are looking at a provincial snowplow driver, and one who is currently employed, or else was employed till very recently, and who has worked on highway 10. Those are the parameters I asked for, and urgently."

He opened his computer. A few moments later, it beeped.

"This is the list," he said, sounding pleased.

Katie glanced at it.

This list was not too long. There were a handful of names on it.

She moved to the desk, filled with resolve. They were going to find the perpetrator.

Leblanc was quicker doing this than she was, but she was determined to equal his speed.

Starting from the top and bottom of the list, they sped through, taking each name and cross-checking it against different databases.

One was the provincial crime stats database, which was very basic but at least would flag for them any criminal record. It was a good place to start.

Next, they matched it against the RCMP investigation records, which were a lot more thorough and had more information on previous arrests and convictions.

As she worked through, Katie started becoming discouraged. Name after name was coming up blank. She reminded herself that only one was needed, and she must not lose focus. The air felt thick with tension. This was now a high-pressure case.

They were tracking down a killer.

Katie searched away. She was making headway slowly, but it was very frustrating.

"How's it going?" Leblanc asked, after a few minutes.

"Nothing," Katie said, shaking her head. Her eyes were starting to blur. She was beginning to feel defeated.

"Me either," he said, sounding discouraged. But just as she'd done, he didn't give up. He turned back to his list and continued.

"It's just a matter of time," he told her, keeping her focus.

And then, he drew in a sharp breath.

"Wait. Here's one," he said.

She glanced at the screen.

Her eyes widened.

At last, they had found a match.

"His name is Armand Lemieux," she said. "He's a local man. Lives here in the area."

Armand was a solid looking man, broad shouldered, with a glowering face.

"He's worked all over this province, and I see he's worked in The Pas."

He was reading from a screen. But Katie's attention was on the other screen.

"He has a record of harassment. His wife, his ex-girlfriend. A neighbor. This guy has issues."

He had been in a relationship with a woman named Evie Kostas, who had a restraining order against him.

Lemieux had been caught on CCTV at the scene of a crime where a woman had been hit with a tire iron. He had been arrested and charged.

Unfortunately, for reasons that were still being investigated, the victim had not been able to identify Lemieux. He'd been found not guilty.

And now, four years later, Katie saw that Lemieux had been working as a snowplow driver for the government.

Privately, Katie thought they were exactly the kind of issues that could escalate into what they were seeing now. The more she saw of the man, the more she could see he was angry. And he had a history of aggression and violence.

Was it possible that they had their perpetrator?

"This is the man we need to talk to," Katie said. She felt a strong sense of urgency.

"We need to speak to him," Leblanc agreed. "And I see he lives a hundred miles away. We could be there in an hour and a half, if we hustle."

She could feel a sense of urgency beating in her heart, like a drum.

Maybe this was the end of the line. She had to hope that it was.

CHAPTER TWENTY FIVE

An hour and a half later, Katie and Leblanc pulled up outside the house that was Lemieux's recorded address. It was in a small, straggling housing estate that seemed to have been built as an afterthought, located in the northern part of a small town.

Thanks to the long drive, it was now early afternoon, and Katie hoped this lead would bring results. Scott would not be pleased if another day went by with no further progress.

A glance around the quiet, snow-laden neighborhood and it was obvious that nowhere was any busier than this little street.

They parked on the road, got out, and walked towards the house. Katie felt a sense of urgency. She had to press ahead. Lemieux needed to be questioned, now.

She was determined to find out if he was the man they needed to speak to.

The home, number three Chestnut Road, didn't look well kept. The yard was un-swept, and snow had piled up outside the front door.

That made her hesitate. Was he even still here? Or perhaps these signs of neglect were because he was on the road so much.

He was a strong suspect. They needed to speak to him. After all, there was his record. The man had a record of violence and aggression, including domestic violence. And he'd been accused of throwing a tire iron and hitting a woman.

The man was a serial offender, who had kept himself out of jail by getting someone else to take the blame, Katie thought.

"Doesn't look occupied," Leblanc agreed.

Katie felt a stab of panic. Were they too late?

But then, she noticed that there were tire tracks and footprints heading around the back of the house. She felt a surge of relief.

Walking around, she saw a car there. It was the type of car she expected a guy like him to drive. It was a Pontiac, black and bulky. It was in good condition, but Katie noticed that it didn't look well kept.

She could hear movement inside the home.

Taking a deep breath, hoping this would lead them to the killer, she walked up and knocked on the back door.

It was opened by a tall, grim looking man with a shock of black hair. He had a big build and a rough face. He was at least six feet tall and had a muscular physique.

"What is it?" he asked, glowering at them.

"Armand Lemieux?" Katie said, glad that Leblanc was standing shoulder to shoulder beside her in case this man got violent. "We're special investigators, following up on a series of crimes."

"And you want Armand?" he asked.

Katie felt taken aback. "You're not Armand?"

The man shook his head briefly. "I'm the property owner. My name's Max Robinson. Armand was renting this place from me for the winter, but he moved out two days ago."

"Do you know where he went?" Katie asked.

"He went south. He said he was going to spend the summer staying with friends in Vancouver, that he was done with the cold for the year."

"So he quit his job two days ago?"

"Yes. He messaged me to say he'd done his last shift and was getting on the road. I messaged him back to say he needed to leave the keys in the house." Max sighed. "He forgot to do that, of course. He couriered them to me from his place in Vancouver when he arrived there. They were delivered this morning so I came here to clean up. He was a slob, but he paid his rent on time." Max shrugged. "It's quite a mess in there," he added.

Katie felt her heart flip-flop. The timing wasn't working out for this strong suspect. He'd been in Vancouver at the time Lizanne had been taken. He could not have abducted her and in fact, if he drove that way, he would have been gone before Sherrie was abducted. It didn't matter that he had a history of violence and had worked in the area until two days ago. He could not have committed the most recent crime.

"Thanks for your time, Mr. Robinson," she said, turning away.

She felt disappointment settle in her stomach. In fact, more than that, Katie felt a sense of desperation.

They had come so far. Now they were back to square one. She couldn't believe that they'd found a solid lead only to have it disproved so quickly. But this was not the time to give up.

She walked down the driveway with Leblanc.

"So, what now?" he asked her.

"We keep going," she said. "We focus on suspects. "We focus on motive. We keep talking to people and keep looking for our man. He's out there somewhere. He's out there, and we're going to find him."

Leblanc nodded, but she could tell that he was discouraged, just like her.

"There are still leads we can follow," she said to Leblanc as they got into the car. "If it wasn't the snowplow driver, it must have been a trucker."

"It's going to be a lot harder to pinpoint a trucker with a criminal record. There's no official list of them, as they work for private enterprise and not for the government departments." Leblanc pointed out.

They climbed into the car. Katie's mind felt as if it was running in circles, picking up and discarding ideas and leads that had already been proven useless.

As she was about to drive off, her phone rang. Katie recognized the number. It was the one she'd dialed earlier, belonging to Lizanne's friend Samantha, who lived in the mining community. Quickly she grabbed the call. She'd given up on Samantha calling her back, but perhaps she had remembered something.

"Hi, it's me again. Sorry I took so long to call you back. I was taking my toddler to the dentist," Samantha replied.

"No problem. Thanks for calling. Did you come up with a location or remember what Lizanne mentioned?" Katie asked.

"Yes, I did. Well, I think so," she said hesitantly. "I've been wondering about calling you. I don't want to give you the wrong information by mistake."

"At the moment, we welcome all information," Katie reassured her.

"I won't get into trouble for a mistake?"

"No, you won't get into trouble."

"Well, I looked at the map, and I'm convinced she mentioned a town with Green in the name. And the only town I can find is one called Greenway. And I think she mentioned a lake. I don't know if that's helpful. Because there are so many lakes in the area," she added uncertainly.

"Greenway," Katie repeated. Leblanc, who had been following the conversation since she picked up, grabbed his own phone and opened his maps.

"It's kind of in the middle of nowhere, north of The Pas. So I think that she might have been looking for a ride near there."

"And what time did you speak to her?"

"At about five p.m. yesterday afternoon."

"Thanks, that's very helpful," Katie said.

"You think so?" Samantha sounded pleased. "I was really nervous about calling. I really hope it helps. I want to feel I've done something for her."

"I hope you have," Katie said, before ending the call.

She turned to Leblanc, who was bent over his screen, busy checking out the area.

"She's right. This is the only town with Green in the name, in this area. So if she remembered right, that gives us a location," he confirmed.

"How far away is Greenway?"

"It's about half an hour's drive from here, I think," he said. "And it's on the shores of a large lake. So that also aligns with the information."

"That's where Lizanne was looking for a ride. I think we should go to that truck stop. They might have camera footage there that could pick her up. Perhaps it's not a busy stop. If it isn't, we could just get the lead we need here."

She felt hope surge inside her again. After all, Lizanne had arrived at this truck stop. It meant they were on the right track. It surely meant they were getting closer to the killer.

CHAPTER TWENTY SIX

Katie and Leblanc drove in silence to the truck stop. Katie's mind was racing with thoughts and ideas, and she was sure Leblanc was equally preoccupied. So much depended on the information that was available at this truck stop, nothing more than a tiny pinpoint on the map, but the place where Lizanne might well have made the fatal decision to hitch a ride with the killer.

Her heart quickened when she saw the sign ahead for Greenway. And there, just beyond the small town, was the truck stop. The bright lights and signage were visible from a long way off, against the gloomy sky.

Checking the map to orient herself, Katie was interested to see that, beyond, the highway branched. The number 10 highway continued straight north, but the number 39 highway branched to the east, joining the number 6 further on.

The truck stop was bigger and busier than she had expected, which she was sure was due to the highway branch, and the fact it served trucks going to a number of different northerly destinations.

The lot was full of big rigs, as well as smaller vehicles. They pulled up at the stop.

Katie felt a sense of excitement as they climbed out. She took a look around.

It was freezing cold, a temperature that seemed to penetrate right to her bones. The icy air was tinged with the fumes of diesel from the idling trucks.

There was a rest stop where ranks of trucks were parked. There was a gas station, and there was a diner and small general store.

"I guess we start there, and see what we can pick up in terms of camera footage," Katie said, looking in the direction of the diner and general store.

She walked over to the stark, tin-roofed buildings. Stepping inside, a waft of warm air, tinged with the greasy aroma of fast food, billowed around her. The diner was busy. An unsmiling waitress was circulating, assisting men on their own, who were likely truck drivers, as well as families and a few people who looked like tourists.

Katie walked up to the counter and waited until the store attendant had finished serving a customer. Then the mustached man glanced in her direction.

"We need your help, if you don't mind. We're police detectives, following up on a series of crimes. Can we speak to the owner, please?"

The man looked surprised. "I am the owner, so I'll help you. I'm Dave Morris. I think I heard something about these crimes. People were talking about women being abducted?"

"That's correct. We believe one of the victims might have caught a ride with the killer at this stop."

"Here? No way. At my truck stop? When would that have been?" he asked, sounding incredulous.

"Yesterday evening sometime," Katie said. "I have a photo of the victim here. What camera surveillance do you have set up?"

He made a face. "Not enough, I'm afraid. This is not usually a high crime area. People come in to eat, to get supplies, and then either take the number 10 or 39 highways. We have cameras at the gas station, and at the exit point. Unfortunately I don't have any in the diner or the store, so it's vehicles only that are monitored on the footage."

"Do you recall seeing Lizanne?" Katie showed him the picture on her phone.

He stared down at it, and then shook his head. "I don't recall seeing her. But we have been very busy here."

"It's surprisingly busy," Katie agreed. "Is it always so busy?"

"This season is always full of activity. It's because we're one of the major stopping points for the ice road truckers. I would say the biggest one of all, as from here they can take about four different routes. They usually follow the number 10 highway north for a while, and then take one of the ice roads that are open this time of year."

"The ice roads?" she asked. Katie knew about them, but hadn't realized that they were so easily accessible from this point. Misunderstanding her, the owner explained as if to a tourist.

"They're the routes to the remote settlements in Manitoba that don't traverse formal roads. The drivers use temporary routes across frozen lakes, and through icy terrain that is only navigable when it's deeply frozen. They're a lifeline for the remote communities, the oil rigs and mine workers that need fuel and equipment, as well as the more remote grocery stores and restaurants that need fresh food supplies during winter. Getting road freight up there is big business, but risky, too."

"So what months do these truckers operate?" Katie confirmed. She was starting to see a picture and wanted to check whether the information would link up.

"It's a short window of time. Here in Manitoba, the ice roads usually open in early January, and will continue for as long as it's frozen, usually either mid-March or late March. At the moment, some routes are already getting dangerous with the ice starting to thaw," Morris said.

"Is that so?" Katie asked.

"Yes. It's a hard job and they're tough people. They drive in very risky conditions, and once they're on the ice routes, there are obviously no truck stops or maintenance stops on the way. So they have to be able to repair their truck, drive in long hours of darkness, and also very often without cell reception for a lot of the time."

"So basically, these men spend a prolonged amount of time out of range, and out of contact of any other people?"

Katie exchanged a glance with Leblanc. She could see that he, too, realized how the dates of the crimes tied in with the ice road trucking calendar. Given that this was one of the busiest hubs, she was starting to see a picture. The pattern of killings matched up perfectly with the opening of the winter roads.

Their criminal was an ice road trucker. Now, she was certain of it.

"Where do they get their supplies from?"

"The Manitoba truckers usually take supplies through from Winnipeg. That's the major hub, as far as I know, and they have a few other depots along the route that they use," the owner said.

Finally, Katie knew, they had him. Undoubtedly, this trucker had passed through the stop at the time Lizelle had been looking for a ride. And that meant that his vehicle would have been captured on the camera footage. Now, it was simply a case of checking.

"We need to take a look at your footage. All your footage, from five p.m. yesterday, through to midnight." Given the approximate time and place of Lizanne's death, Katie knew that window of time would cover the truck driver leaving.

"That's going to be a lot of trucks. A lot of vehicles," the owner warned. "I'll download all the footage and bring it to you on a USB drive, if you want to take a seat in the diner. I'm not sure how useful it will be."

"That's perfect, and it will be useful. We're going to narrow it down."

As the owner headed into the back room, Katie explained to Leblanc in a low voice.

"We look up every single number plate and trace the vehicles' ownership. We find out which trucks are owned by the ice trucker companies. And we ask them to confirm who the drivers are, and if they run to and fro along that route regularly."

"Then we'll have an idea of the ice truckers who were here, who could have taken her," Leblanc said.

"It makes so much sense, in terms of how this criminal could abduct these women and hold them for hours. He's holding them while he drives the ice roads. There's no risk of being found out. Not when you're in such an isolated area."

"Yes, that's our answer."

"If we look at the timeframe when Lizanne was asking for a ride, we might end up with only a handful of possibilities Then we check their backgrounds and go after them, in order of how strong a suspect they are."

"We can sit right here in the diner," Leblanc said. "Let's liaise with Scott and see how fast we can get some results back from the footage, combined with the ID of these drivers."

As Katie took a seat in the diner, she couldn't help wondering if the killer himself had sat here too, overlooking the forecourt and with a view of the store, keeping an eye out for any potential victims.

They were going to catch up with him; Katie knew they could. In a couple of hours, if all went well, they would know the identity of the man committing these crimes, and might be on his trail.

CHAPTER TWENTY SEVEN

Rosanne Smith pushed the Start button of her car yet again, feeling frustration seethe inside her.

Yet again, the engine turned over weakly and then died away.

This damned car! It had given her nothing but problems ever since she'd bought it second-hand last year. And now, it was refusing to start.

Of course, it was doing so at the worst possible time. Her dad, who lived alone in a small town north of Winnipeg, had broken his leg in a bad fall yesterday. He was going to be wheelchair-bound for a while, and thirty-year-old Rosanne had said she would drive down there to help out. He'd need someone to help him get around for a few weeks, to cook some meals for him, to keep him company until he was more mobile.

Her dad had sacrificed a lot for her. He'd put her through college; he'd been a tower of strength when she'd doubted herself. Now, she had a good career as a translator, and it was time for her to help him in turn.

But the car was not cooperating.

She dialed roadside assistance and waited, tapping her fingers on the dashboard.

"Hi, I need help. My car just died and it won't start."

Rosanne watched as an eighteen-wheeler accelerated past, snow flying from the tires. She really didn't like being here on the road. It felt exposed and unsafe.

"What make and model of car is it, ma'am?" the man on the phone asked.

"It's an old Ford Explorer. White. And I'm on highway 10, about fifty miles south of The Pas."

"Ma'am, we have a big storm front coming in and we're trying to get as many calls through as possible. I'm sending someone out to you right away but they'll probably take about forty-five minutes to reach you. Are you in a safe place meanwhile?"

"I guess so," she said. She wasn't in any danger, as long as the trucks saw her. At least her emergency lights were working.

"You stay safe, Ms. Smith. Stay inside the vehicle. It's cold out."

"Sure, thanks." She hung up.

The car was already freezing. Forty-five more minutes? And then she was getting a tow? That didn't sound promising. She might not make it to her dad today.

Anxiety started gnawing at her stomach. If only there was something she could do. At that moment, headlights gleamed behind her, bright in the snow on this gloomy day.

Another truck was passing, another big, shiny eighteen-wheeler. Only this one was slowing down. Lights flashed. Brakes hissed. It was pulling to a stop behind her, in the emergency lane.

Puzzled, Rosanne watched as the driver jumped out and hurried over. Swathed in a scarf, a hat, and sunglasses, she could barely see his face.

"Are you okay, ma'am?"

She wound the window down. Cold air billowed in.

"I'm fine, thanks."

"You need me to take a look at the engine for you? I know a bit about cars. I might be able to fix it."

"I've got a breakdown truck arriving," she said.

He frowned. "When are they coming? It's not safe here. A woman on her own, you shouldn't be waiting here alone."

"They're getting here in half an hour," she said, shortening the timeframe slightly in the hope that they would, actually, arrive earlier.

"Let me take a look first. I may be able to get it going for you."

Rosanne hesitated. She appreciated the fact that he was trying to help out, but a strange man in this isolated location? It was hard to trust.

"I'd better wait for them, now that I've called them," she said.

"I'd hate for you to be stuck here for hours," the man said.

"I'll be okay. They'll be here in thirty minutes."

"I'm not going to leave you here like this. Come on, let me have a quick look under the hood."

"Thanks, but I'd rather wait," Rosanne insisted. She didn't trust random guys who thought they knew how to fix cars. She didn't want it ending up being worse.

"They'll leave you here in the cold. They could be a long time yet if this storm comes. What if your engine freezes up and they can't shift it? They won't be able to tow you, then."

She hesitated, wondering.

He was trying to help. Maybe he could get her engine going again. Maybe she should let him. She knew the road was dangerous, and she didn't want to be stuck out here.

"Come on, ma'am. How about I take a look at it? I've got some tools in my truck."

"It's really fine," she said firmly. That was one thing her dad had always taught her. No meant no, no matter what. She had help arriving and she had decided to wait for that help.

That was something else her dad always reminded her of. Would a man treat you differently if you were another man? In this case, Rosanne thought he would treat her differently. He would not be so pushy, so insistent on helping.

It was something to be wary of, her father's wisdom reminded her, the words resounding in her head.

Did he really just want to help, or was there another reason for these insistent offers?

"Thank you. You're welcome to wait with me if you are worried about my safety. But I've booked a tow and I'm going to honor the booking," she said firmly.

"Ma'am, I'll gladly do that. I know you probably think I'm being out of line. But if you were my wife, stuck here, I'd be concerned. I'll wait in my truck until help comes. Honk the horn if you would like hot coffee," he smiled.

Now Rosanne felt bad. She felt like she'd judged him wrongly when he was trying to help. She looked like an ungrateful and horrible person.

Maybe he was just trying to be nice. And it was cold and windy out here. She was frozen to the bone already.

"I'm sorry," she said quickly. "That was rude of me. If you're worried about my safety, you're welcome to wait here with me."

"I'll do that."

He walked back to his truck, his feet scrunching through snow.

Rosanne closed the door, feeling deeply relieved to shut the icy air out. She was now shivering from that little exchange through the open window.

She settled back in her seat, aware of the truck's headlights behind her, wondering what she could do to pass the time.

And then, there was a shadow at the window, so sudden she jumped.

He was back!

The trucker was back, grabbing at the door handle. Fright surged inside her. It was locked. She hadn't undone the central locking. He'd been trying to pull the door open.

Rosanne screamed as the man tugged on the door. Trapped in her car, she began honking the horn.

No, wait. That wouldn't help. Not on this empty, icy road. Nobody would hear.

She needed to call for help. To call the police. Urgently, because her instincts were right, and this guy was out to harm her not help her.

She grabbed her phone, shaking with fright, feeling utterly trapped, but as she did, she saw out of the corner of her eye that he was wielding something big and metallic.

A moment later, the window glass exploded inward as she cringed away, yelling in fear.

"No! No!" she yelled, trying to fight him off, knowing it was hopeless, her defenses were breached, this game was over now.

He reached in.

Something touched her neck, and a jolting burn lanced through her.

Then, she knew nothing more.

CHAPTER TWENTY EIGHT

Leblanc felt more confident about this case, now that they had the ammunition he needed to catch up with the killer. He was armed with the facts that would allow him to start the hunt, and he felt excitement surge inside him at the thought they were now close.

On the red-checked tablecloth of the diner's table, it was all set out in front of him.

The camera footage allowed him to see the number plates of every truck that had departed during the critical time when Lizanne could have been taken.

That was running on his laptop. He paused as each truck came into view on departure, identifying each registration number, entering it into the document he'd created and immediately sending it through to Scott and the task force team in Sault Ste Marie. This was a team effort and speed was the priority. He felt grateful that he had the rest of the team helping with the research on that side.

Right now, he just wanted to get a result. He had to catch up with the killer, and he was going to do it.

Katie was right there beside him, her face focused and intent. He knew how well they worked together. Barely even needing to speak, they were each anticipating and taking forward the other's moves. He felt a surge of gratitude that he'd earned her trust. And perhaps, in time, if their relationship continued, it would also be her love.

Katie was currently busy calling the ice road companies who worked this route. There were five of them that were active and doing business in Manitoba. Each one, during the season, employed twenty or more drivers, and most of the drivers took this route north. So it was important to collate the different information streams, matching the number plate with the trucker's ID, to pinpoint the likely suspects.

Then, there was a third stream of information they needed.

Criminal records.

There had to be some history behind this behavior, Leblanc knew. An individual like this was deeply troubled and he was certain they would uncover some record of violence or another precipitating event.

"I've got the information from the ice road companies," Katie said, completing her last call. "They are sending me all the names of the drivers they used, who are active and working on that route at the moment. And they've also linked the drivers up to the trucks that they were assigned to, so we can match the names and number plates and then see who passed through here at the right time."

"And then, we can cross-check for their involvement in past trouble," Leblanc said.

Scott and the other members of the task force team were in charge of that research, which would require being linked to several official databases and was more easily done on site at the task force headquarters.

The technology of CCTV, satellite tracking, and the internet would lead them to the killer.

The truck stop owner bustled past their table again. He was clearly feeling guilty about having been the pickup point for a victim to be taken. He looked concerned, and was carrying yet another pot of free coffee, and a selection of candy bars, to fuel them while they worked.

Leblanc felt grateful for the food and the caffeine.

He entered the last number plate, sent the final portion of the list to Scott, and topped up his cup. His stomach felt tense with expectation. Scott and his team had been working for an hour already. Any moment now, there might be a match.

His phone rang and he grabbed it, his heart quickening.

"I have something," Scott said.

"What is it?" Eagerly, Leblanc put his phone on speaker as Katie leaned over to hear.

"It's a trucker called Doug Alder, who has been driving that route regularly for two years now. He would have passed through this stop going north, within the window of time Lizanne was looking for a ride."

"What's his background? Does he have a record?" Leblanc asked.

"Yes. He has a record. Seven years ago, he did time for manslaughter. He's been clean since then. No further offenses, no trouble with the law, but as you know, that might only mean he hasn't been caught. I'm going to send you all his personal details now."

Leblanc checked the list. Alder worked for a company called Northwestern Haulage.

Katie, who'd been communicating with the companies, got on the phone to her human resources contact at that company immediately.

"I have one more question for you, if you don't mind," she asked politely. "Doug Alder. Do you know where he is at present?" She waited, listened.

"Thank you," she said. "And can you tell me, on a personal level, has Mr. Alder been a troublemaker in any way? Has he had any disciplinary hearings, any complaints, anything on his employment record?"

She waited again, and this time her eyebrows raised.

"Thank you so much," she said gratefully.

She cut the call and turned to Leblanc. " The manager I spoke to said he's a problem employee. He's belligerent, there have been road rage incidents, he takes too many risks. He's currently on a final warning. And something else, Leblanc. He's very secretive. He has skipped routine inspections at the depot more than once. He won't allow anyone to offload his truck until he's given permission. They've been wondering about him for a while, and wanting to investigate. It sounds like this is our man."

"And where is he now?" Leblanc asked.

"He's on a two-hour break at the depot in a town called Grafton, stocking up with food and supplies for a short detour to the south of that town. Then he will travel to Winnipeg, collect a load of fuel, and go far north on a longer trip again."

"So for now, he's at the depot in Grafton?"

"Yes. So we need to get there as soon as we can. If we can reach him at the depot before he leaves, it would be best case for sure," Katie said. "

Leblanc was already out of his chair, packing up his things and flinging them into his bag.

They needed to get to that depot before Alder left. Given the swift and escalating pattern they were seeing, the risk was exponential that if he got on the road again, he would seek out and kill another victim.

*

Half an hour later, Katie and Leblanc pulled up outside the depot in the small town of Grafton, which was half an hour to the south of where they had been.

The depot was nothing more than a small warehouse, one of a string of other industrial looking buildings, situated on the only tar road in town, close to the highway. It was a cold looking place, that seemed to have a lot of industrial activity. Leblanc guessed this town must have a population of a few thousand.

A couple of cars were parked outside the warehouse.

Leblanc felt tension fizzing inside him as he approached.

He and Katie walked through the doorway, which was partway open. From outside, the building smelled of oil and damp. Inside, it was quiet, but the silence was somehow more unsettling than if the place had been bustling.

An attendant in overalls, who had been packing shelves, strolled over.

"Can I help you?" he asked in rather unhelpful sounding tones.

"We're police, looking for Doug Alder," Leblanc replied.

"It's in connection with an investigation," Katie added.

The man shrugged. "Okay," he said reluctantly. Leblanc sensed that, like so many in these remote areas, this individual didn't have much love for the police. "Come this way."

They followed him out, around the car park, and along a paved path that led to the back of the warehouse.

They got there in time to see Alder loading up a few cardboard boxes into the back of his large, shiny rig.

As he approached, Leblanc eyed out the man. He was tall and strong, with a shock of dark hair. He had a beard that was more stubble than anything else, and Leblanc thought his eyes were shifty.

"Doug Alder?" Leblanc said.

"What is it?" he asked suspiciously, turning to them.

"We're police," Leblanc began.

But before he could give any more details, Alder's face changed. His features tensed. He jumped down from the back of his truck.

"Hey!" Leblanc cried.

But Alder wasn't sticking around. He took off running, pounding along the path that led out of the warehouses, and into the back of the town's industrial area beyond.

"Catch him!"

Leblanc took off after him, his shoes slipping on stray fragments of ice, the breath freezing in his lungs. This man was guilty! Now, they had to catch him before he managed to escape into the industrial area beyond.

Ice slipped and splintered under his feet.

"Stop!" he shouted. "Stop!"

But the only response was the echo of his voice.

The back of the warehouse was separated from the main town by a few small buildings that offered little cover. Alder was in good shape. He was running fast, fast enough to get away from them. He looked like he was running with a purpose in mind, and Leblanc was utterly sure that purpose was to evade them for as long as he could.

He couldn't risk this case being stalled. He could not risk having this man flee out of town in another vehicle and pick up a victim along the way. He had to catch him now, before he could make a getaway.

The trucker turned the corner, sprinting toward a paved path that led behind the industrial area, that led to a stark looking housing estate beyond.

His footsteps echoed on the concrete. He zigzagged around trash cans, sprinted across a patch of icy ground, and sprang for a chain-link fence that was the barrier between the industrial side of town, and the housing estate.

He scrambled to climb up, and then he was gone over the fence and pounding down the walkway beyond.

"Stop! Police!" Leblanc shouted.

He scrambled over the fence, hearing Katie's footsteps as she raced behind him.

Leblanc's heart was racing. He had to keep going. He had to catch him. There was no way he could let him get away.

He flew around the corner, feeling as if everything was at stake here.

And there was the man, sprinting down the walkway, his head down. This was going to be his best chance to catch him. Maybe his last chance.

With all his remaining strength, Leblanc put on a burst of speed. Charging ahead, he managed to make a flying leap and tackle the fleeing man.

Leblanc managed to grab hold of the man's pants leg as he landed hard on his stomach. The air was knocked out of him. He'd managed to bring Alder down but not hold onto him. The man sprawled onto the paving with a curse, but was already scrambling up.

Leblanc was breathless, winded, and aching. He struggled to get to his feet because Alder was already on the attack. He was grabbing for a weapon, picking up a discarded fence post. The metal rail looked solid and heavy.

He swung it at Leblanc, with vicious intent in his eyes.

The steel bar whooshed toward his head, heavy and lethal. Yelling in fear, Leblanc ducked and rolled, managing to avoid it. The bar swung through the air, crashing to the ground, making a terrible metallic clang.

Then Leblanc scrambled back, fumbling to unholster his gun, hoping he could get it out in time, because already this madman was lifting the bar again for another try.

But before Alder could swing the iron bar again, Katie arrived, pounding up at a run. She had her gun out. She skidded to a stop a few paces away, gasping for breath, but her gun hand was rock steady.

"Drop that weapon," she called. "Now. Immediately. Or I will shoot."

There was ferocious intent in her words.

Alder looked at Leblanc and then his gaze swung to Katie.

He grimaced in anger.

His muscles tensed, and his eyes narrowed. Katie tightened her trigger finger as she tried to read his body language. If he was going to act violently and try to attack, she'd have no choice but to shoot.

And then, as if changing his mind in the moment, he dropped the bar. It clanged on the ground.

As he released it, Leblanc leaped forward and grabbed his wrists. With hands that were shaking from the sheer adrenaline rush of the chase, he handcuffed him.

After a pursuit that had used up all his reserves of energy, they finally had their man.

Now, they needed to get him into custody and link him up to the crimes. Leblanc knew this case had to be rock solid.

With a flicker of fear, he remembered the snippet of conversation he'd overheard Scott having.

They could not afford any mistakes at this point, not when their task force was under scrutiny.

CHAPTER TWENTY NINE

Alder sat in the small interview room in the Grafton RCMP department. He was glowering at Katie and Leblanc. She sensed negative energy exuding from him.

She had a strong feeling that he was being protective and defensive. She could see it with every movement he made. His body language was confessing truths that Katie doubted they would easily get from the man himself.

He was going to be tough to crack. This was exactly what they did not need.

She leaned forward. "Mr. Alder," she began. "We need your cooperation with a serious investigation. A murder investigation. Are you willing to help us?"

He didn't say anything. He just stared back at her. Of course he wasn't willing, she thought. Why would he willingly participate in something he knew would take him down and see him land in jail?

She waited, hoping that silence would prove effective in wearing him down.

Eventually, he started showing signs of unease. He shifted his weight, he looked around the room, he stared at his handcuffed wrists. He was uncomfortable now with the silence.

"Okay. What do you want?" he asked at last. He sounded impatient.

"Hitchhikers have been abducted and murdered. It's happened this season. This winter. We're focusing on truckers who have been out on the roads, and traveling a specific route. That includes you. You've been in the area at a time when a confirmed abduction took place, and you have a record."

She stared at him, waiting to see if he would start to crumble under the weight of the proof she was offering.

"This is ridiculous," he finally said. "I'm a trucker. I'm on the road all the time. I work in ice conditions. I focus on my job, and getting it done right. You ask my bosses. I don't have time to be killing people."

"Why did you run from us?" Leblanc asked him.

Alder's eyes narrowed. "I didn't have to stay around to take the heat for something I didn't do," he said.

"You're protective about your truck. You don't allow people near it while you drive. What's the story there?" Katie asked.

"The truck is my livelihood. If goods get stolen from inside, I'm responsible and I'll be fined. Have you seen the contracts we have to sign? We're liable for everything, man. Why would I allow people near it?" he asked.

"We have seen your police records. You have assaulted people before."

"Those charges were inflated, way out of all proportion. I was the scapegoat, make no mistake," he blustered.

Katie was discreetly monitoring her phone during this interrogation. Two RCMP officers were checking the truck, and another two had been dispatched to conduct a search of Alder's home and personal vehicle. She was hoping that they would soon send through their findings.

She was certain that they would find evidence linking him to these crimes. As soon as there was proof, she was going to confront him with it and see if he was ready to spill.

But, as she glanced at her phone, a message came in that she did not want to see.

"The suspect's truck seems clean. No sign of a taser or a firearm, and we've searched the entire vehicle. Also, no evidence of anything that could be used to contain or restrain a victim," the officer had sent.

Katie felt a thud of disappointment.

Evidence would pave the way for a strong case. Without evidence, they were going to have to rely on Alder himself. And he was not showing any signs of breaking.

She glanced over at Leblanc. His face was grim, his eyes serious. He was not happy with this development.

"You have a record of assault," Leblanc insisted.

Alder looked like he was going to explode. He banged his hands on the table. "I didn't do it! You're out to get me. You want to tear my life apart, I can see. But I am innocent! I just want to earn a living."

"We're not done yet, Mr. Alder," she said. "We know that there's more you're not saying. We'll get to the bottom of this."

Stubbornly, he insisted, "I didn't kidnap or murder anyone. I've got nothing to hide."

Katie could see he was not going to talk. She could tell that much from the way he was acting.

"It's funny how people who say they have nothing to hide, are always hiding something. Maybe you should tell us. It will go much better for you that way, than if we find out," she threatened.

"You can't make me talk," he spat back.

She waited. She was determined to get him to talk. She didn't care how long it took. But he stared at her, like he was daring her to go farther.

At that moment, Katie's phone started ringing.

She stood up and headed out, seeing that the caller was the RCMP officer who'd gone to search Alder's home.

Behind her, she heard Leblanc resuming the questioning, keeping the pressure on Alder because they were under pressure of time to solve this.

Katie hoped this officer had uncovered something. Because she didn't like the way this case was heading. It seemed to be devolving into a black pit of missing evidence. She'd seen cases like this fall apart before now.

At present, the evidence against Alder was only circumstantial and she desperately needed solid facts to bolster it.

"Any news?" she answered as soon as she was outside the room.

"We're here at the suspect's home," the officer replied. "Agent Winter, we've done a preliminary search of the house, and also his private vehicle. We have found evidence."

"What evidence?" Katie drew in a sharp breath. Finally they were getting somewhere.

"We've picked up on some banned substances. I'm wondering if he was transporting uppers, GHB and LSD and selected pharmaceutical tablets when he did his northern runs. Because there are stashes of all of these in the cupboard under his sink, and also in his vehicle's cubbyhole."

"That could be. Please log the evidence carefully," Katie said.

She ended the call, took a deep breath, and buried her head in her hands. This was not the answer they wanted. Their suspect was guilty without a doubt. But it seemed not of the crime they had brought him in for.

She had a very unappealing choice.

Either press charges regardless and hope that he ended up being found guilty of both, and that more evidence came to light.

Or else, keep looking for someone else.

The problem was that there were no other truckers who had departed the truck stop within that timeframe who had a criminal record, or any trouble with the law at all. None of them were even new to the job; she'd checked that. All had been working at least two seasons.

Was her theory totally wrong?

Self-doubt clenched at her. This case was critical. Their unit was under scrutiny, and she was failing to come up with any suspect that would convince a jury of their guilt.

Katie paced down the corridor, feeling cold air filtering through from outside. A rustle of the breeze told her that weather was blowing in, fast. Perhaps these dark clouds would bring a snowstorm.

Or perhaps not. Casting her mind back, Katie remembered that at similar times of the year, similar clouds could also bring an unseasonable rainstorm, and a sudden temporary thaw.

And thinking of the weather reminded her that there was more than one way to look at everything. Clouds could mean rain, but also snow. They could bring a thaw, or a harder freeze.

Turning her focus back to the suspect again, she suddenly wondered - what if she was wrong, but right?- What if she had the right idea, but just needed to seek out different factors?

There was something strange about this criminal's behavior. She knew that already. But she hadn't found him yet, and that meant she was missing something critical. So she needed to do what every investigator hated. She needed to acknowledge she had overlooked something important, and go back to try and find it.

But what was she searching for?

Maybe not a criminal record. Maybe a triggering event.

Think of the rain, not the freeze. Think differently, she encouraged herself.

Perhaps she needed to seek for something that had changed in the life of one of these ice road truckers, between last season and this season. Something she had not been told about because she hadn't asked about it.

The right questions could lead her further, and as Katie dialed the number for the first of the ice road trucking offices, she hoped that she would be able to ask them this time.

Because this case was teetering on the edge of failure.

CHAPTER THIRTY

"It's me again. Agent Winter," Katie said to the human resources manager who picked up her call. This was her second call to the first of the five companies she'd called earlier.

"Can I help you?" the woman replied, sounding guarded.

"Your truckers. You said there were none among them with criminal records."

"That is correct. We have a policy about hiring such people."

"Did any of your staff, that you know of, have any other incidents occurring toward the end of last year or this year that went onto their employment record?"

"Such as what?" the woman asked, puzzled.

"Perhaps there was a death or a trauma in the family and they had to take compassionate leave? Perhaps they suffered a crime incident or had a breakdown, or even some sort of physical injury? I know trucking's risky. Perhaps someone had an accident?"

Katie really was trying to cover all eventualities here because she didn't want the woman to miss out on telling her about a potentially triggering event.

"No, ma'am. I am pretty sure that none of that happened," the manager replied. "We had a couple of minor collisions but thankfully nothing more serious, and I can tell you it's always a relief when we end the season without any major accidents."

"Are you sure? Were there any incidents where you sent staff to the hospital?"

"The only one that I know of was Sandra, one of our warehouse managers. She had to take time off for an operation after she injured her leg when she slipped outside the building. And one of our truckers broke his arm snowboarding, but he was obviously off duty at the time."

"Thank you," Katie said.

She called the second company.

"It's me again, Agent Winter," she said.

Quickly, Katie repeated her request. This manager had been the most unhelpful of the five, she remembered. She sounded all out of patience this time.

"No, ma'am, we did not have any incidents last year to speak of. We're very happy about that. We want to keep it that way," she said, in tones that told Katie she was unwilling to continue this discussion in more detail.

Katie thanked her, ended the call, and continued down the list.

The third company she phoned, the receptionist also had nothing significant to report.

"We had one truck lose a wheel on an icy slope. The trucker managed to bring it to a stop without too much damage. He was fine. Bruised, if I recall, and the truck was dented in places, but nothing else. The load was intact."

"Thank you," Katie said.

There were only two left, and she was getting nervous.

She called the fourth one. The receptionist she'd spoken to here had sounded young and bright.

Again, Katie repeated her story.

"Oh, yes," the woman said. "I wasn't with the company then. I only joined this year, but I heard about the incident. It was very sad."

"What happened?" Katie asked.

"One of our drivers went off course and ended up going into a lake that was thawing. He had his wife riding with him. That's allowed, by the way. Company policy is that spouses and girlfriends may ride along. But it went wrong, and she unfortunately drowned. He was injured, but managed to get out of the cab."

"Is that so?" Katie said. That could well have been a triggering incident. The pieces were looking similar. "And did he work for you again after that?"

The receptionist sounded uneasy. "It was right at the end of last season. He'd already signed on for the new season and he was contractually bound to complete the assignment. I don't think he wanted to, but like I said, the contract was in place and he didn't contest it. He's driven with no problems since then."

"What's his name? And his truck's number plate?"

"Let me look. His name is Rick. Rick Corby. Here's his number plate."

As she read it out, Katie turned to the laptop and called up the information she'd been gathering earlier.

Quickly, she scanned the list.

Her heart accelerated as she saw that this was a match. This trucker had left the truck stop in the window of time when Lizanne had been reported missing.

"Where is Rick Corby now?" Katie asked.

"He's on the road. He's completed a few short-distance drops, and now he's picked up supplies from the midway depot in Grafton, and is heading far north doing a delivery to one of the northern settlements. Fuel and perishables. He would have started that trip four hours ago from our depot and I think he'll be at his first stop in about three more hours. Then he has one more stop, another two hours further north."

Katie breathed out.

At last, they had their suspect. She was certain it was him. Now, all the threads were coming together. The man could have suffered a psychotic break after the trauma. The company had enforced the contract terms, or maybe he'd just been too broken to contest them. Either way, he'd driven again, but as a result of the trauma, he'd veered into a murderous cycle. Perhaps he was wanting company on the route, or to replace his wife in his mind.

At least they had time to locate him, Katie thought. They could prepare carefully for this arrest, and make sure that he was taken down in a methodical way.

Katie closed her eyes for a moment and tried to picture how the next few hours would play out.

They would locate the trucker, she told herself. They would take a helicopter to a point ahead of him, coordinate with the closest municipal RCMP departments in that settlement, and then wait for him when he rejoined the blacktop roads. They would surround his truck, stop him, and then they would move in, quickly, and grab him.

It would be risky. He had already proved that he was volatile and unpredictable. He was armed. But as far as takedowns went, Katie had seen far worse.

This would be a textbook arrest, she promised herself.

But as she mentally mapped out what they would need to do, she heard hurried footsteps behind her.

Turning, she saw Leblanc rushing through. He was gripping his phone and looking anxious.

"I took a break from questioning Alder," he said. "I went to get some air outside, and as I stepped out, I saw Scott was calling me," he said. "There's been another victim taken. At least, it appears so. Scott has only just put two and two together."

"What?" Katie gasped. "How did this happen?"

"It was a woman whose car broke down, name of Rosanne Smith. She called for roadside assistance, but when they arrived, they found her window smashed and she was gone. It came through on Scott's radar a while ago, but it was originally reported as a smash and grab. They have now realized she's actually missing and it's been reclassified as a possible abduction."

"Where was this?" Katie felt cold inside.

"It's on the number 10 highway north. Just past a town called Three Peaks. It was about three hours ago already."

It was him. Katie looked at the map, sketching this ice trucker's route from the time he would have left

Katie knew it.

He wasn't just taking hitchhikers. He had escalated, and was actively hunting for victims.

He was now storming over the icy roads, across frozen terrain miles from anywhere, on the way to his destination. He had this woman locked inside his truck, imprisoned there somehow.

And, if his pattern was the same as it had been, he would kill her before he reached the next stop. Then, he would dump her body somewhere, cover it with snow, or tuck it out of sight.

There was no time to spare. No time to plan. Not anymore.

"He might already have killed her, but if he picked her up recently, maybe he's keeping her a while. She might still be alive, but she won't be for long. He will kill her before he gets to where he's going," Katie said.

"We might be able to save her yet," Leblanc agreed.

But the earlier plans Katie had sketched out in her head were now totally redundant. If this woman was going to be saved, she knew, they had to act as fast as possible. It would be risky. Methodical planning was all the way out of the window as they raced against time to save her life.

She was going to have to put her own life on the line, and put her career on the line, also.

She realized, if this case went wrong, there was a risk it might jeopardize the task force's future. But if they did nothing, then without a doubt, this woman would die.

She had to do it. She had to save the victim. That was all that mattered.

CHAPTER THIRTY ONE

"Tell me what you did today," the driver asked. There was only silence from the cage in the seat behind him.

She wasn't answering, wasn't speaking to him at all and he couldn't work out why. Had he done something wrong?

He could hear her breathing from the cage, but no sounds of distress. He thought he should offer her some food and drink, but he didn't want to let her out.

He didn't want to let her out of her cage. But she was his friend. He knew that. Memories of previous conversations floated into his mind.

Had they been with a different person? He thought so, but that strange blockage was in his thoughts, preventing him from going any further with this chain of logic.

"Do you want some coffee?" he tried.

Still nothing. He couldn't even hear her breathing. Glancing around, he saw her out of the corner of his eye.

She was there, where he was keeping her.

He was heading north, into the cold. But the weather was changing. The snowstorm that had been threatening seemed to be blowing away. The air suddenly felt lighter and breezy. These heavy clouds held something different.

To his surprise, cold rain began pattering on the windshield.

Instinctively, he checked the tract of ice ahead, with faint tire marks showing where other drivers had gone, almost invisible in the darkening afternoon.

Rain meant thaw. Thaw meant danger.

Suddenly, a memory surged. A memory of a lake, black as night in the darkness. He'd judged it wrong. The ice had shattered.

The rainwater was spattering up against the windshield now.

"No," he whispered.

It was the lake again. The lake that had trapped him. He was approaching the same stretch. Treacherous. There were warm currents under the lake. He remembered tragedy, trauma, loss. But he couldn't remember why.

He remembered plunging in, and how the truck's body had grated and shrieked as the ice embraced it. He remembered screams.

Terror rose up inside him and the truck swerved, causing him to correct course hurriedly. He realized that he couldn't let himself think this way. He couldn't let himself remember.

That was the past, it was over, and he was in control now. And he had a woman with him. He had a friend. But he was convinced that this wasn't the right person. He'd done something wrong and she wasn't talking to him. As soon as he could, he was going to pull over. Put an end to it. He would start the search again.

For now, though, he had to concentrate. The weather was making it difficult to see the road. The rain was spattering down hard.

He could hear the growl of the engine. His cab was warm and safe. He was going as fast as he dared in the conditions, but it never felt fast enough.

Should he take a shortcut? Was that what he'd done before?

He thought back, but the memory wouldn't come.

For a moment, he considered his trip. He was in a hurry this time. It was hard to keep up with the schedule. This weather brought so many challenges. But he was going to make it. The question was whether he should stop now and do what he needed to do, to complete the cycle. Before he reached the lake.

Because the woman wasn't speaking at all and that meant she might as well be dead.

He'd wanted company and he was getting none. So perhaps it was time to kill her.

The driver realized he'd been musing out loud, muttering his thoughts into the emptiness of the silence.

Thoughtfully, he slowed the truck. This was an isolated area and there was nobody to see what he was doing. Even though the rain was falling, he could still hide her under some half-melted snow. The elements would claim her.

He checked the mirrors and saw that there was nothing behind him. Nobody was pursuing him. Nobody knew what he was going to do. They were supposed to drive in convoy but in practice, that didn't always happen. He rode many of his routes alone.

Nobody could stop him.

But, at that moment, a small voice called out from the cage behind him.

It was the woman. Speaking to him at last.

"Are you okay?" she asked. Her voice was small and shaking.

A strange emotion gripped him. Relief. She was speaking to him at last.

"Yes," he said. "I'm okay."

"Can I have something to eat?" she asked. "I'd like something to eat. And then let's speak. I want to speak to you. I want to hear what you have to say."

He looked around, smiling, because it was all going to be okay. He had his company. She was speaking to him now and that meant he could wait until they'd crossed the lake, follow his original plans to kill her before he reached the drop-off point. He felt glad she could live another hour.

"Candy?" he asked. "You want candy?" There was a chocolate bar on the dash.

He reached back and handed it to her through the cage.

It was a small, weird pleasure to hear her open it.

"Thank you," she said. Her voice was unsure, but at least it was a voice. It brought back echoes of his past.

He glanced into the rearview mirror, but he didn't see the woman in the cage.

All he could see was his wife. She was there, in the back. Her eyes were closed, but she was sleeping peacefully.

It was better to push on now, and get past the ice before it began to melt. The ice was always dangerous, and he had to be careful.

It seemed a shame to kill her at all, he thought suddenly, but he knew it had to be done. He didn't remember why he had to kill her. But he knew that before he reached his destination, she would die.

CHAPTER THIRTY TWO

The helicopter blades whipped the air as Katie and Leblanc flew north, heading for the last known location of the truck they were hunting. Rick Corby had last checked in with head office three hours ago. He'd been on the highway 10, heading north, but had been about to branch off from the highway to the east, and follow the ice roads over a series of frozen lakes, that would lead him to the first of the northern settlements beyond.

They had no further coordinates.

"We've just got to look out for him," Katie told Leblanc.

The helicopter was being flown by a seasoned RCMP pilot. Katie felt glad of that because there was another complication. The dark gray clouds that had been looming did not hold snow. As she'd instinctively realized, they heralded a rush of warmer air, and now it was raining heavily.

"The rain is affecting visibility, badly," the pilot said through tight lips.

Katie stared down at the gray, turbulent landscape below. The truck roofs were white. Spotting a white truck, against a pale, frozen landscape crisscrossed by ice roads, with driving rain obscuring their vision, was the equivalent of a needle in a haystack.

She was determined to try.

They had been flying in silence while they searched. The landscape was icy and unforgiving and visibility was poor, and closing in.

There were no other planes, no other helicopters. They were on their own, one team, single-handedly trying to locate this truck, in an area where it could be anywhere.

"They usually take the demarcated routes, but sometimes, to save time, they'll choose other routes. And although they are supposed to stay in a convoy, and in radio contact, especially when crossing the more remote and dangerous areas, from what we've seen, they often don't do that," the pilot explained.

Katie was sure Rick Corby would not do that, because he had a reason for branching off.

He had a passenger in his truck and he was going to use the vast, snowy expanses of wilderness to hide her body when he shot and killed her. If they could not prevent this, Katie knew she would live with the guilt of a final life lost, for a long time to come.

"Over there!" Leblanc exclaimed suddenly. Katie heard the note of hope in his voice as he pointed down. "What's that?"

Raindrops spattered the glass and the pilot banked, trying to come in from another direction for better visibility.

She looked.

In the distance, she saw an oblong of white against the ice. It was almost impossible to make out. She was grateful Leblanc had spotted it.

"Go for it," she shouted. "That's the truck. It must be him! It's off route, but it must be!"

"Go around," Leblanc said to the pilot. "Fly behind him. I don't want him to see us."

The helicopter banked, then swooped over the landscape.

"What's our plan?" the pilot said. "How are we going to stop this guy?"

Katie thought fast.

Her initial plan had been to follow the truck, so that he would know he had a police presence in the air and it would prevent him from slowing and stopping to kill her.

But she had to think ahead, to think as if she was him, with his damaged, psychotic mind.

He might decide not to stop. He might change his plans and shoot the woman while he drove. Katie knew she must be in the cab with him because the back of the truck would be too cold and too far.

She was his possession, the replacement for something he had lost. He'd have her in there with him, close by.

Within range of his gun, for sure.

She had to think of every possibility, and plan for every eventuality.

"I think we need to descend in front of him," she said. "We need to surprise him and force him to slow down and stop immediately. The quicker we can do that, the less time he will have to think about killing her. His focus will be on us."

"Sounds good. Risky, but good," the pilot said, as Leblanc nodded his approval.

But as they flew lower, descending in the rain, Katie saw that this plan was not going to work.

Because the trucker had already heard them. Through the driving rain, the sound of their blades must have been loud enough for him to pick up.

Katie drew in a horrified breath as the truck swerved sharply.

He was going to try and run. He was going to get away from them. But in this rain, with the water pounding down onto the ice, every deviation from the route represented a risk.

Right now, though, he was a desperate man. He was delusional. He wouldn't care about the consequences of his actions. Even though he was trying to get away from them, Katie wondered if in some strange way, he was also seeking death.

They were flying lower now, coming up behind the truck, and Katie watched in horror as the truck drove over a ridge in the ice. The truck slewed, rocking violently, swerving on the road.

If it rolled, his hostage might end up dead. Even if it didn't roll, a blow out at this speed could be disastrous. Her life was at stake.

"Do we have ropes? Let's get the ropes ready," Katie said. If the truck crashed, they'd have to fast-rope down there and access the cab to try and get her out. It was incredibly dangerous, but nothing about this operation was safe or normal in any way.

The truck was racing ahead now, at an insane speed, plunging over the uneven, windblown sections of ice. She could hear the crash and clatter and knew what effect this might have on the rapidly thawing surface of the lake. Katie saw chunks of ice and snow flying up into the air as the truck swerved wildly.

Katie opened the helicopter door. Blowing wind and sheets of rain battered her. Could she try now, she wondered. Could she get in the window of the moving truck? She didn't think so. Such a mission would be disastrous, but she didn't know what else to do.

"Should I try?"

"It is going to be dangerous!" Leblanc protested. "Katie, this is too big a risk. There has to be a safer decision."

"We have to do something!" she argued. "And I can't think what else we could do."

"Then let me go," he pleaded. She could see the tension in his body, the worry in his eyes.

But she wasn't prepared to risk him, either.

"You're not going alone. We both go," she decided.

Leblanc nodded reluctantly. Now, she could see he understood there was no other way.

"I'm flying as low as I can," the pilot assured her.

The truck's roof was only about twenty feet below. It was plunging and fishtailing over the uneven ice. Gripping the rope, Katie prepared herself for the descent, knowing that Leblanc would follow to provide backup. Together they might be able to overpower him.

Nerves fizzed through her. She'd fast-roped before, in training, but never in a life-or-death situation like this. She took a deep breath, preparing for the dangerous ride down and then the confrontation with the killer, all from a precarious point, and at speed.

But then, as Katie watched in horror, she saw the ice begin to shatter.

"No! Turn away!" Katie screamed, as if he could hear her.

The truck was careening out of control now, unable to correct as it began to slide.

The ice shattered.

Katie saw it happen in slow motion, as if time had slowed. The ice fractured, broke, smashed apart under the truck's inexorable weight.

And cab-first, the ice truck plunged down into the chilly waters with an enormous roar.

CHAPTER THIRTY THREE

Katie couldn't believe what she was seeing. The sight of the heavy truck smashing through the ice was horrifying. Sheets of ice ricocheted high into the air. Below, the dark waters heaved and churned with the impact.

She had no idea how deep this lake was, but it was a huge lake, and the truck was at least half a mile from shore. It was likely to be deep enough to swallow the truck, and its occupants, without hope of rescue. Unless they got to them fast enough.

"We've got to go and get her out. Now! I'm heading down!" Katie yelled. There was no time to waste. The truck was already sinking fast, plowing into the shattered chunks of ice.

The rope felt slippery in Katie's hands. The rain was blinding. Grabbing it hard, she launched herself out of the helicopter, gasping as the rain sheeted at her.

The rope was unbelievably slippery, slick with the rain. Her hands slipped on its rough length and she clung to it, knowing that if she lost purchase it would mean almost certain death. The wind was buffeting her, feeling like a giant hand that was trying to wrench her away from her precarious handhold.

Drawing on all her courage, she forced herself to confront the terrifying circumstances. She forced herself to loosen her grip. Allowed herself to slide, plummeting down toward the raging waters. She blinked away rain, blinded by a sudden gust.

The truck was close. Too close. She grabbed the rope tightly, knowing she was coming in too fast, risking injury. For a heart-stopping moment her already-numb hands slipped. And then, she found her grip and was able to slow her speed.

The truck's cab was already partially submerged. She lowered herself into the icy water. They needed to smash a window. That was going to be the only way.

She took out her gun and used it as a battering ram, smashing the barrel against the glass.

It splintered, and then shattered. Katie kicked the glass out of the way with her boots as water rushed in. Now was the time to make a leap of faith, and hope she could complete this rescue before the truck sank, taking her down with it.

Letting go the rope, she grabbed hold of the truck's doorframe and tugged at the passenger door.

Behind her, Leblanc rappelled down to join her. Together, using all their strength, they managed to wrestle the door open.

Now, Katie was hanging onto the cab of a rapidly sinking truck. The lake was deep. Inch by rapid inch, the water was claiming it.

Where was she?

She could see no sign of Rick Corby in the bubbling water. The driver's side was already under. But he was not the main priority. The main priority was his prisoner.

Looking behind the seat Katie could see a wire crate. It was already partially submerged under the rising water. Her breath caught in her throat as she realized that was where his captives were imprisoned. The door was secured with cable ties.

She could see the woman's hands, clinging to the wire. She was hanging on, still alive, still fighting.

Katie took a deep breath and plunged under the icy water, knowing she didn't have much time, that every moment that passed brought a greater risk that Rosanne might drown.

The water was so cold it took her breath away. Paralyzingly, heart-stopping cold. She almost gasped involuntarily at the shock, and had to force her lips closed. Already, her body felt numb. Her arms felt like they didn't belong to her.

She fumbled on her belt for the knife. Forced herself to grasp the handle. Clumsily, she sawed through the cable ties, one by one.

Leblanc joined her under the water, tugging open the wire door.

Eyes stared at her, and in them she saw a spark of consciousness. This woman was still alive.

Katie grabbed hold of her arm and dragged her out into Leblanc's waiting grasp. Water frothed and bubbled into the cab. Shards of ice grazed her. The cab was almost completely under water now.

They had her, though. They had gotten her free. Leblanc wrapped his arms under hers and kicked strongly, out of the door and up to the lake's surface.

But as Katie followed, a hand grabbed her from below.

The shock was so great that water whooshed into of her lungs. It was Rick Corby. He was fighting her. He was pulling her back, his fingers locked around her leg. In the dark, turbulent water she could see his face. See his eyes. In them, she saw doom.

He wanted her to die with him, to complete the deadly cycle.

Katie didn't have much time or air. She kicked out as hard as she could, with all the force she could muster in the freezing water, her body already shuddering from the icy cold.

She kicked and kicked, but Rick's grip was strong. He didn't want to let her go. He wanted to drown her, too. Katie saw it in his eyes. His expression was twisted and desperate. He was willing to take her down with him.

And she might not be able to fight him off. She struggled, thrashing and kicking, but he was powerful, and he wasn't giving up. He held on, and the cold water was starting to paralyze her. Her lungs began to burn. In a moment, she knew she'd have to take in a breath, and then it would all be over.

It was so cold Katie thought her blood might freeze right in her veins. Her legs were already cramping. She knew she had to break away or she was going to die.

Katie kicked again, with all her strength. She struck out, hitting his face.

Her foot slammed into him. She put her whole weight into the blow. It was all she could do. Her last attempt.

Rick's grip weakened. He flailed in the water. She feared he was going to try and grab her again and pull her back down to the arctic depths. But she swam for the surface, as hard and fast as she could, knowing that only speed could save her from this monster.

With her lungs bursting, Katie breached the surface and gasped in a huge gulp of air. She'd done it, she'd escaped him. There was the helicopter above them, and they now needed to lift this victim to safety so they could try and resuscitate her.

Katie grabbed the rope and twisted it around her and Leblanc, hanging on with all her might as the helicopter carefully lifted the three of them.

The helicopter moved, slowly, taking them across the lake's frozen surface. Katie watched the fractured ice go by below her.

There was the shore, there were the flat, snowy slopes, now drenched with rain, that were safe.

The helicopter lowered again and Katie let go her death grip on the rope, sprawling down onto the snow.

She grabbed the woman, who was coughing and choking. She was alive. She had survived. Katie held her, helping her, trying to shield her from the streaming rain as she coughed and spluttered the last of the water from her lungs.

"You're okay," she said. "You're okay."

"Thank you – for saving me," Rosanne choked. "I tried to – buy time. To talk to him. To delay what he promised to do."

"You did well," Katie said, squeezing her hand, even though she could barely feel her own fingers. They were all drenched and shivering. There were blankets in the helicopter and she could use them to get this woman warm and dry.

Leblanc was directing the helicopter in to land.

Now that the victim was safe, Katie knew they needed to go back and urgently get the killer.

But when she looked at the lake again, she saw to her astonishment that the truck had disappeared.

It had sunk, far below the surface of the lake. The patchy ice had flooded back over the water, and she could not even see exactly where it had gone under.

Without a doubt, the killer was dead, drowned in the same icy grave that had claimed his wife's life.

The circle was completed. He would take no more victims. And they had been in time to save his final captive.

EPILOGUE

The rain that had swept over the northern areas, bringing with it a fast thaw, had dissipated. Weak sunshine added brightness to the morning, and Katie thought it was going to be a perfect early spring day.

She stood with Leblanc at the Winnipeg airport.

With the case closed and all the paperwork correctly signed off, they were not flying straight back to Sault Ste Marie. Instead, she and Leblanc were making a quick detour to New York, to follow up on a lead regarding her sister's disappearance.

Mrs. Ingham, the woman who had rented a house to Gabriel Rath, was back in town and she had agreed to speak to them. She said she had information on where he had gone.

Katie felt nervous and expectant, not knowing what the information would be. But she felt glad to have Leblanc standing next to her.

They had spoken deeply last night. They had agreed that they were not going to deny the feelings between them anymore, and that they were going to let their relationship develop and see where it led, even though they would keep it private for now, between the two of them. Life was short, they agreed.

This last case had proven to Katie that you never knew when somebody you loved might be ripped away from you. It was important to seize the moment.

"But I want a favor from you," Leblanc had asked. "I want to help you with your sister's case. I want to make a difference in your life. If you have a challenge, let me help you to solve it."

Having him with her was incredibly comforting, because Katie had no idea what this information would be, or where it would lead them.

"Perhaps it will be Rath's new location," Leblanc theorized. "We must hope it will be."

"Even if it isn't, we could still take another walk around town and ask more people," Katie said, even though she knew their time there would be limited and that Scott was expecting them to report for work early the following morning.

"We can do that," Leblanc confirmed.

At that moment, Katie's phone rang.

She picked it up, feeling curious and surprised, because it was her old boss from the FBI unit, Senior Special Agent Andrews. She hadn't spoken to him for months. Why was he calling, she wondered.

"Andrews! Good to hear from you," she said in greeting.

"Katie," he replied. "Listen, I wanted to tell you, that if you are making a decision in the near future, I want you back here, okay? Don't you dare take any other posting." There was a hint of humor in the words, but otherwise they sounded very serious.

"A decision?" Coldness flooded her. What was he saying? He sounded as if he knew something she didn't. "Why should I need to do that?"

She hoped he would tell her. After a pause, he did.

"Your task force has been too effective," Andrews explained briefly. "You've been taking the glory away from people who want the political points. One person in particular is pulling strings behind the scenes. I heard from a connection high up, that your task force is almost certainly going to be disbanded, and soon. I believe the decision will be made in the next few weeks."

Katie felt herself tensing. The next few weeks?

Their task force, destroyed, disbanded, and all due to nothing more than petty political ambitions?

She'd seen such fallout happen before, but had never thought it would affect her own unit to the extent of obliterating it.

Coldness settled in her stomach.

She wondered what she could do to fight it, and acknowledged there was probably not much.

It was within her powers to take down a killer, regardless of the danger. But to fight in the political playing field? She didn't have the clout or the experience to do that.

Now, she felt as if all she could do was wait for a hammer blow to fall.

"Thanks for letting me know, Andrews," she said. "I'll rejoin you if the unit is dissolved, I promise."

She could see Leblanc looking visibly worried at her words.

Katie knew that in the next few weeks, her entire landscape might change. She and Leblanc might end up separated, never to see each other again.

There might be no future for her here, in this place where she had chosen to build a future and had embarked on a new relationship.

With uncertainty surrounding her in every direction, Katie felt helpless.

But then she resolved she was not going to take this lying down. She was not! She might be just an agent, but she would fight for the preservation of their unit.

She was going to learn more about this decision, she promised herself.

She was going to investigate who was behind it, and how it could be stopped.

There must be a way, she told herself, with resolve cutting through her despair. And if there was, she was going to find it.

"I loved this book! Fast-paced plot, great characters and interesting insights into investigating cold cases. I can't wait to read the next book!"
—Reader review for Girl One: Murder

"Very good book… You will feel like you are right there looking for the kidnapper! I know I will be reading more in this series!"
—Reader review for Girl One: Murder

"This is a very well written book and holds your interest from page 1… Definitely looking forward to reading the next one in the series, and hopefully others as well!"
—Reader review for Girl One: Murder

"Wow, I cannot wait for the next in this series. Starts with a bang and just keeps going."
—Reader review for Girl One: Murder

"Well written book with a great plot, one that will keep you up at night. A page turner!"
—Reader review for Girl One: Murder

"A great suspense that keeps you reading… can't wait for the next in this series!"
—Reader review for Found You

"Sooo soo good! There are a few unforeseen twists… I binge read this like I binge watch Netflix. It just sucks you in."
—Reader review for Found You

<u>PROTECT ME</u>
(A Katie Winter FBI Suspense Thriller—Book 8)

Molly Black

Bestselling author Molly Black is author of the MAYA GRAY FBI suspense thriller series, comprising nine books (and counting); of the RYLIE WOLF FBI suspense thriller series, comprising six books (and counting); of the TAYLOR SAGE FBI suspense thriller series, comprising six books (and counting); and of the KATIE WINTER FBI suspense thriller series, comprising nine books (and counting).

An avid reader and lifelong fan of the mystery and thriller genres, Molly loves to hear from you, so please feel free to visit www.mollyblackauthor.com to learn more and stay in touch.

BOOKS BY MOLLY BLACK

MAYA GRAY MYSTERY SERIES
GIRL ONE: MURDER (Book #1)
GIRL TWO: TAKEN (Book #2)
GIRL THREE: TRAPPED (Book #3)
GIRL FOUR: LURED (Book #4)
GIRL FIVE: BOUND (Book #5)
GIRL SIX: FORSAKEN (Book #6)
GIRL SEVEN: CRAVED (Book #7)
GIRL EIGHT: HUNTED (Book #8)
GIRL NINE: GONE (Book #9)

RYLIE WOLF FBI SUSPENSE THRILLER
FOUND YOU (Book #1)
CAUGHT YOU (Book #2)
SEE YOU (Book #3)
WANT YOU (Book #4)
TAKE YOU (Book #5)
DARE YOU (Book #6)

TAYLOR SAGE FBI SUSPENSE THRILLER
DON'T LOOK (Book #1)
DON'T BREATHE (Book #2)
DON'T RUN (Book #3)
DON'T FLINCH (Book #4)
DON'T REMEMBER (Book #5)
DON'T TELL (Book #6)

KATIE WINTER FBI SUSPENSE THRILLER
SAVE ME (Book #1)
REACH ME (Book #2)
HIDE ME (Book #3)
BELIEVE ME (Book #4)
HELP ME (Book #5)
FORGET ME (Book #6)
HOLD ME (Book #7)
PROTECT ME (Book #8)

REMEMBER ME (Book #9)